SYMPHONY FOR A SURGEON

Only Julie Singer's friend Lynn knew the true reason for her being a nurse at St George's, but even with a confidante, training for her SRN became increasingly difficult. Not only did her associates find her impossible, there was also Adam Rich, a dedicated and demanding surgeon. Then there was Doctor Susie Tulip who was determined to marry Adam, by fair means or foul – and, alas, Susie stumbled on Julie's secret.

SYMPHONY FOR A SURGEON

Symphony For A Surgeon

by

Margaret Chapman

Dales Large Print Books
Long Preston, North Yorkshire,
BD23 4ND. England.

British Library Cataloguing in Publication Data.

Chapman, Margaret
    Symphony for a surgeon

    A catalogue record of this book is
    available from the British Library

    ISBN   1-85389-978-X pbk

First published in Great Britain by Robert Hale Ltd., 1981

Cover photography R.J.B. Photo Library by arrangement with Rene
Brown

The moral right of the author has been asserted

Published in Large Print 2000 by arrangement with Robert Hale Ltd.

Dales Large Print is an imprint of Library Magna Books Ltd.

Printed and bound in Great Britain by
T.J. (International) Ltd., Cornwall, PL28 8RW

ONE

How could she admit it, confess?

How could she reveal the true reason for her being at St George's? Julie stuffed the letter back into her drawer, then shakily she began to change into her nurse's uniform.

What could she do?

Her late uncle's solicitors in New York now wanted a written report on her first year's work in hospital. A report from Matron! It was imperative that they should have this.

But how could she possibly explain, confess to Matron that hers had been no eager commitment to nursing but only a desperate attempt to gain the £50,000 left to her by an eccentric old man. She was to be the chief beneficiary, but there was a proviso. Before this money could be handed over by the trustees she had to qualify as a State Registered Nurse.

A report from Matron! Julie drew another quick breath and again dismay filled her blue eyes. Matron would think she was nothing but a money-grabbing opportunist. And a liar to boot. But how could she have told Matron about her career as a concert pianist, that when her father died she had been forced to give up her studies at the London College of Music? And then, out of the blue, a letter had arrived from Middlemass and Sinclair, offering both challenge and hope. An SRN certificate and she could not only provide for her mother and young brother but also return to her own studies.

Sober-eyed, Julie clipped back her smooth brown hair and then pinned on her first-year nurse's cap. She looked shocked, she thought, and she frowned unhappily at her reflection in the long wardrobe mirror. Shattered! Somehow she had to come up with something. She had got through one year of her training and she was determined to get through the next two.

'Darling,' her mother had protested miserably, 'I don't think you should do it. We can manage. Julie, you were never meant to be a nurse. You haven't the stamina.'

'Mum, I have,' Julie had argued. 'Believe me, it takes stamina to get through a concert. Besides, I've made the decision. I've written to that hospital in the north.'

Still protesting, her mother had flopped on to a chair and grieved, 'Darling, you're must too sensitive. Oh, I do wish we'd never heard of your wretched uncle again. He was quiet enough when he was alive. And if he hadn't had that accident and been forced into a hospital we would never have heard of him again.'

'He was impressed,' Julie had laughed back. 'He left that hospital quite a gift. Of course, he probably fell for a nurse – the bad old bod. And lucky for us. And, you know, Mum, this training may come in useful one day. Anyhow, you can't cheat destiny.'

'You can't fool a hospital matron either,' her mother had warned. 'She'll soon find out that you're not the type for the work.'

Her mother had been wrong; her first-year report had been good. If she had fooled Matron, then she had certainly not let her down. But now this letter from Middlemass and Sinclair. What was she to do? Nervously, Julie picked up her keys, hurried out of the room, locking the door behind her, then swiftly she made her way along the corridor in the Nurses' Home – Virgin's Alley.

She was late! And it was theatre morning on the gynaecological ward. Professor Rich had a long list. Sister Grey, middle-aged and round, would be stotting about the ward like a ping-pong ball. List Days on Eleven were notorious; everyone dreaded them.

Breathlessly, Julia hurried through the warm conservatory and, making her way up the wide marble staircase, she started along the main hospital corridor for Eleven. Then, as she entered the annex corridor to the ward, Sister Grey shot out from her office.

'Oh, there you are, Singer!' she called shrilly. 'I thought you might have inadvertently died. I suppose you know it's List Day.'

'Yes, Sister. I'm sorry, Sister.'

'You haven't time to be,' Sister Grey shrilled. 'Into the ward, Nurse. The list is on the desk. We're about half-way through.'

Her face flushed, her heart thudding, Julie made her way to the end of the ward where Staff Nurse Watson was making up a theatre bed.

'What kept you?' Staff Nurse Watson complained under her breath. 'Theatre nurse has gone to theatre and the junior's not back until eleven. You'd better finish making up this bed. I'll give the next patient her pre-med.'

'Yes, Staff.'

After acknowledging a quick consoling smile from the woman in the next bed Julie got on with her work. Then Freddy the porter came blithely down the ward, calling, to the irritation of Staff Nurse Watson, 'Next for the roundabout.'

'It's Mrs Fairless,' Staff called grittily. 'Bed six. She's ready.' And with a flick of her hand, she ordered, 'Nurse Singer, give Freddy a hand.'

Julie did not care for Staff Nurse Watson's manner but she obediently hurried to assist the porter to get Mrs Fairless on to the trolley. A big, noisy woman, she now lay back like a pregnant whale; helpless, touchingly vulnerable. Patting the woman's plump hand, Julie encouraged, 'You'll soon be all right now, Mrs Fairless. Before you know where you are you'll be back in bed and it will be all over.'

Too drowsy to speak, Mrs Fairless managed a faint smile, while the thin angular woman in the next bed chirped cheekily, 'You're right, Nurse. No one could keep her down for long.'

Freddy whistled as he wheeled Mrs Fairless away, and Julie returned to finish making up the theatre bed. As she folded in the blankets she wondered again what reason she could give Matron to persuade her to write out a report on her first year's work. Could she say her mother wanted it? No, that was ridiculous. She would have to come up with something better than that. But what?

'Nurse!'

It was Staff again, beckoning impatiently to her. Truly, List Day on Eleven was an appalling day, thought Julie.

'The airway,' Staff Nurse went on, the moment Julie reached the bedside. 'Make sure to remove it first.' And, 'Hand that scoop over, nurse. Put her head on to the side.'

Julie was in time with the scoop but only just. Staff Nurse Watson tightened her lips impatiently. 'You'll have to be quicker than that,' she snapped. 'Take the airway to the sluice.'

There was no time, for just at that moment, the houseman, David Whittaker, a hearty, rugby-playing type, came striding down the ward, his red curly hair escaping from his theatre cap, his face flushed with anxiety. 'The Prof's about to take off,' he blustered, his eyes on the heavy-limbed, sharp-eyed Staff Nurse. 'Who the devil sent down that last case? She came without her case-sheet. And, God forbid, her teeth were still in! The Prof wants to see the nurse who imagines he can work with such a handicap. Now!'

Turning scarlet, Julie met Staff Nurse's hard, accusing glare.

'You?' David Whittaker gasped, frowning unhappily at Julie. 'Come on, then,' he groaned. 'You'll have to face him.'

On their way downstairs to the theatre David Whittaker caught Julie's arm. 'You'd better fasten your seat-belt,' he warned. 'You're about to be blown sky-high.' And because Julie had no pert reply and because her eyes were alarmingly blue, he went on uneasily, 'Just don't say anything. Just take it. You're not the first nurse to come a cropper with the Prof. And somehow I think you'll live to tell the tale.'

As they approached the double doors of the theatre Julie swallowed painfully. She had no excuse. She had simply been pre-occupied with her own affairs. But now her head swam and she felt as though she was walking on jelly. After a year without incident was she now destined for a black mark?

Adam Rich was waiting in the Anaes-thetist's Room next to the Operating Theatre. He was a big, handsome man, and he was wearing casual trousers and a cool short-sleeved shirt. The gown he had thrown off lay over the back of a chair. Spruce, freshly barbered, this confident surgeon waited to reprimand the nurse who had by her carelessness slowed down his whole programme. A dedicated man, disci-plined, he could not tolerate incompetence. Usually he chose the nurses he wished to work for him and, as a rule, everything ran smoothly. Yet, here he was waiting for a case-sheet! Here was the anaesthetist, the theatre staff, his mob of insensitive students all waiting ... for a case-sheet which should have arrived with the patient.

The swing doors opened and David Whittaker and Julie came breathlessly into the small ante-room. Adam Rich drew himself up to his full six feet and stared hard at the girl who stood before him. She was trembling visibly and her raised eyes were incredibly blue. She also had a sensitive, intelligent face. Frowning, he went on considering Julie for a few moments. As light as a bird and not more than nineteen, he assessed. Neat ankles, neat wrists and particularly nice hands. A wide, lovely mouth.

And lips which had every reason to tremble. 'Nurse,' he began, deepening his already ocean-deep voice, 'you will perhaps tell me the object of Mrs Fairless's visit to my theatre. If possible, I prefer not to work in the dark.'

At this scathing but controlled remark, Julie could only stare back unhappily at him. She wanted to say something but her tongue seemed to have locked. She felt such a fool! So idiotic! Tears of self-depreciation brightened her eyes.

'Your name, Nurse?'

'Singer. Nurse Singer,' David Whittaker put in uneasily.

'Dr Whittaker,' Adam Rich instructed smoothly, 'perhaps you would be kind enough to tell the anaesthetist to begin.'

'Yes, sir.'

'I'm sorry, sir,' Julie burst out the moment they were alone. 'I'm dreadfully sorry, Professor Rich. I haven't any excuse. I got flustered.'

A pause, then a loaded question. 'You fluster easily, Nurse Singer?'

Unnerved by his keen scrutiny, Julie nevertheless managed to brave his widened eyes. 'No, sir,' she assured in a small, soft voice. 'I do not. This morning something occurred to upset me.'

'Did it? I am sorry, Nurse.' Adam Rich found himself fighting hard to restrain a smile. 'And what do you imagine happens when something occurs to upset me?'

Helplessly, at his mercy, Julie bit her lips and clenched her hands. 'I am sorry,' she said again. 'I was careless. I apologise.'

'Then return to the ward, Nurse,' he said with a sudden abruptness, 'and get on with your job. That will allow me to get on with mine. That's all.'

'Thank you, sir.' With a sigh of relief, Julie turned to go. She hadn't been blown sky high! The Prof hadn't even sent her to Matron. He had a heart. This big, handsome, masterful surgeon had a heart.

When Julie got back to Eleven, Staff Nurse Watson was waiting. 'What happened?' she asked eagerly. 'I suppose you've got to report to Matron. And that won't do you any good. Professor Rich has a lot to say in this establishment.'

Julie laughed back. 'You make me sound like a marked woman,' she said in a pleased tone. 'Actually, the Prof was very generous. He merely told me not to forget the case-sheets in future. He never mentioned Matron.'

'Then you're lucky,' Staff Nurse shot back airily. 'And you can bless Dr Tulip for this concession. They say the Prof's in a marvellous mood these days. He's crazy about Dr Tulip. And it appears that she's crazy about him.'

'Dr Tulip?'

'The new lady doctor on Women's Medical. She's really something. That woman has everything going for her. Money, looks, brains – and now Professor Rich.'

Julie looked thoughtful for a moment, then Staff was saying, 'Come on, this isn't time for gossip. The hysterectomy from bed four is back and she's on a drip. You'll have to keep an eye on her for a while, Singer. I'm going to first dinner but, if you need anyone, Sister will be in her office. The junior is due back from her weekend off. She can do the round and the washes with the auxiliary.'

Another examination of the patient in bed four and Staff Nurse Watson set off for dinner, a look of satisfaction on her face. Julie sat down on the chair by the bedside and stared anxiously at the ashen face of the woman in the bed. Mrs Stone had undergone major surgery and she had lost quite a lot of blood. Yet, Julie reckoned, this same woman would be sitting up for her breakfast the next morning and on the third morning she would be on her feet again. Miracles *were* performed on Eleven. The professor was a remarkable man. Also a man to make any girl's senses thrill. This latter thought came out of the blue, and as though embarrassed by it, Julie stood up again. Again she checked Mrs Stone's pulse; lightly, she raised the sheet to ensure that there had been no haemorrhaging. Then, satisfied, she stood with her back against the radiator.

She would confide in her friend Lynn, she suddenly decided, as her own problem loomed large again. Lynn was bright, she might even come up with some idea. And Lynn could keep a secret. They had been friends since their first day in training school. Had she not been afraid of embarrassing her friend, she would have told Lynn about her uncle's will long ago.

How quiet the ward was, she thought, as her gaze now followed the bone-thin junior and the middle-aged auxiliary, who looked rather like an overfed duck in her big flat shoes and tight white coat. There was always an atmosphere on List Day. To some extent everyone was subdued. And now she was the only nurse in the ward, the junior and auxiliary having gone off to find Sister.

No, she wasn't! Suddenly Julie's heart was thudding warningly, the colour rising from her throat. Professor Rich had slipped quietly into the ward. He was striding towards her. She had to find Sister!

'How is she?' Professor Rich enquired gravely. He stopped to consider Mrs Stone, then the drip-flow.

Then he turned to Julie and she looked

into velvet, dark eyes. 'She's fine...' she heard herself falter ridiculously.

'Fine?' The eyes were darkly stern now and they bore down into Julie's. 'Nurse,' he said levelly, 'this woman has just had a hysterectomy. She can't have been out of theatre for more than an hour. And you tell me she's fine?'

His words held a stinging rebuke which left Julie stricken. 'Her pulse is steady, Professor Rich. She's getting her colour back and she's not haemorrhaging.'

'Thank you, Nurse.'

'I'll tell Sister you're here, sir.'

'There's no need, Nurse. I'm just having a quick look round. I'll be back at four.'

'Yes, sir.'

A pause and then Adam Rich turned to consider Julie. 'This hasn't been your day, has it, Nurse?' he said in a deep, almost teasing voice. 'Still, I'm glad to see that you have stopped shaking.'

Again, Julie felt her heart flutter, but again she merely clenched her hands and firmed her lips. There was nothing she could say; she was in a bad position. She did, though, raise her eyes and give him a grave stare.

Adam Rich strode away, a faint smile stirring his sharply etched mouth. Pale and girlish, sensual and terrified of him. Small and neat, still and modest. They certainly got a variety of nurses on Eleven. It was this little creature's voice he liked; it was so soft, so musical.

'Professor Rich! I didn't know you were doing a round!'

It was Sister Grey, and she gave Julie a swift, condemning stare.

'It's all right, Sister,' Adam Rich called smoothly. 'The little nurse managed quite nicely.' As he swept past her, he added, 'Everything seems all right, Sister. I'll be back to do a round at four.'

The little nurse! Catching his words, Julie firmed her lips even more tightly. Then Sister Grey was calling, 'Nurse Singer, you can go to dinner now.'

After lunch Julie and her friend Lynn

walked back together through the hospital to the Nurses' Home, stopping only when they got to the post office to enquire if there was any mail for them.

Sister Cole was on duty; she glanced over her specs along the shelves and then shook her head.

'Well, we didn't really expect any, did we?' Lynn laughed, and they passed on to the lift, which they took to the second floor.

'Not really,' Julie began again, as she unlocked her door. 'But come in, Lynn. I have some news for you.'

'News? For me? Oh, good! What is it?' Lynn, a tall, leggy girl with amber eyes and masses of copper hair, flung herself down on the bed. 'Wait until I take my shoes off,' she added, and she kicked them off.

'We've both got the afternoon off,' Julie started again. 'Are you going out, Lynn?'

'I was thinking of having a round of golf. But, come on, don't keep me in suspense. What news?'

'Lynn,' Julie began carefully, sitting down

on the small spartan bed beside her friend, 'there's something I should have told you long ago but I had hoped to keep it to myself.'

'Well, thanks! What's changed your mind?'

'Lynn.'

'It's trouble ... I can see by your eyes.'

'Not exactly.'

Lynn took off her cap and shook out her curls. 'I'm all ears,' she said and she sat back against the wall. 'What's wrong, Julie? Fire away.'

'In short,' Julie said, standing up to nervously pace the small room, 'I'm a fraud, Lynn. I'm here on a false pretence. I never wanted to be a nurse. I still don't want to be a nurse. You remember I told you I was studying at the London College of Music.'

'On the ding-dong – yes, I remember. You were always going to give me a tune.' Something in Julie's expression subdued Lynn, and again she shrugged and said, 'All right, carry on. I won't be frivolous.'

Julie paused now to stare gravely at her

friend. 'Lynn,' she began again, carefully picking her words, 'when my father died I had to leave my studies. My mother had to go back to teaching. As you know, I have a brother who is still at school. It was terrible! I got a job in an office and loathed it. And then, out of the blue, an uncle who I'd never set eyes on left me £50,000...'

'What!' Lynn sprang on to her feet and then flopped back on to the bed again. 'What! £50,000! You're having me on, Julie. I don't believe it.'

'It is true, Lynn.'

'Then you're rich! We're rich,' Lynn laughed excitedly.

'Just a minute,' Julie went on in a sober tone, 'I haven't got the money yet, Lynn. There was a proviso.'

'Oh, no! You don't get it until you're ninety?'

'Please, Lynn. I don't get it until I have my SRN. That was the provision made. And now you know why I'm here at St George's.'

Lynn was silent for a moment, then she

asked, more calmly, 'Then, what's happened? Why did you decide to tell me?'

'Lynn, the solicitors in New York want a report from Matron on my first year's work at St George's. I just can't tell her the true reason for my being here.'

'No, you can't,' Lynn asserted. 'She'd boot you right out.'

'I know.' Julie lowered her eyes. 'I thought you might think of something. For my mother's sake and my brother's, I must get that money, Lynn. Also, it will give me the chance to carry on with my music.'

After a sigh and a long stare at her friend, Lynn said, 'Do you really hate nursing?'

'No, I don't, Lynn. Honestly, I'm quite happy here. But it's not my world. I can never be myself at St George's. I have a talent, Lynn, and I've got to use it. I must! I must!'

Lynn sighed again, then she stood up and said with her usual directness. 'Then I'll write a report for you. I'll forge Matron's signature.'

Julie stared back at Lynn in amazement. 'You wouldn't?' she breathed, her heart suddenly beating faster. 'You couldn't.'

'Why not?'

'I couldn't let you,' Julie went on protestingly. 'I wouldn't.'

'But you will,' Lynn laughed back. 'You're weakening already, Julie. So now all I need is a sheet of hospital notepaper.'

'Lynn, dare we?'

'I've told you, I'm willing to take it on ... providing you can pay for afternoon tea down town. I'm suddenly off golf, Julie. Let's go down to Charlie's. We can talk about it.'

'Oh, Lynn, I'm so worried. I just don't know what to do. I feel a bit of a cheat. And now I'm asking you, my best friend, to be one.'

Springing away to the door, Lynn grinned and called back, 'Didn't you know, it's wealth and not wits that demands respect, Julie. From now on I'll do anything you say.' Outside the room, she stuck her head in the doorway to exclaim, 'Fifty thousand, did you say? Wow!' And rolling her eyes, 'You won't ever have to pass the cap round.'

'See you in ten minutes,' Julie called breathlessly.

'Are we going in the Rolls?'

'Oh, stop fooling, Lynn,' Julie suddenly burst out irritably. 'You've no idea how worried I am.'

The door closed at last and slowly Julie began to take off her uniform. She just had enough money to pay for their teas.

* * * *

Adam Rich had parked his car just within the gates of the hospital and now he sat back to wait for Dr Tulip to appear. Through the driving mirror he had a clear view of the drive which ran up to the hospital. He was tired and now and again he closed his eyes. Theatre mornings were always grilling. And it certainly seemed his day to be kept waiting. Where was Susie?

Glancing in the driving mirror again his attention was drawn by the reflection of two young girls coming down the drive. They were talking earnestly to each other. One was tall with bright copper hair. The other one ... Adam Rich blinked. Good Lord! the other one was Nurse Singer. Sitting back, he narrowed his eyes to observe them at leisure. In mufti, Singer looked even more vulnerable even though she wore a sensible-looking duffle-coat, from one shoulder of which swung a very lethal-looking bag. She had nice legs and a straight back and her smooth brown hair swayed as she walked. She made him smile. In spite of everything he liked this girl. He remembered she had incredibly blue eyes. He smiled again, wryly, remembering how he had found himself smiling that morning instead of damn well bawling her out.

'Professor Rich,' Lynn said under her breath and as they picked up their steps, 'Did you see his car? He was parked in it. Waiting for Dr Tulip, no doubt.'

'What's she like?' Julie enquired over a tongue which suddenly felt dry.

'The type men want in full focus.'

'The Prof sent for me this morning,' Julie went on, hoping that Lynn had not noticed how the colour had rushed to her face. 'I'd forgotten to send a case-sheet down to theatre.'

'Oh, Lord! You'd get it. The Prof hates carelessness.'

'He wasn't too hard on me.'

'Hmm,' Lynn gave her friend a swift glance. 'I suppose he thought you'd crack up at one sharp word. You do have a fragile air, Julie.'

'It's deceiving, then. I'm as strong as an ox.'

'I suppose you have to be to tackle a piano,' Lynn laughed.

Julie was not listening. As the professor's car rolled by, and Lynn said under her breath, 'Peasants back,' she caught a swift impression of the young woman who sat in the seat next to the driver. A classic profile, blonde, almost white hair, a luxurious fur hat.

'That was Susie Tulip,' Lynn announced as they stood watching the car gather speed. 'I guess she'll never be short of a penny. Or a man!'

Julie hurried on ahead, anxious that Lynn should not see her burning cheeks.

'Hi, wait for me,' Lynn called. 'What's bitten you?' And, falling in beside Julie, she said, 'You're not envious of Susie, are you? You're not going to be short of a penny either. Unless, of course, you're having me on. I still don't know whether to believe you.'

'When we get to Charlie's I'll show you the letter,' Julie said in a strangled voice, and again she hurried on.

'I wonder where those two were going,' Lynn called in an animated tone. 'Perhaps they're off for a few rounds of golf. I've seen the Prof on the course. He looks super. He wears fabulous clothes. No one would ever take him for a hatchet man.'

Charlie's Restaurant was in the city centre and Lynn soon found a table by the window. The sun was shining, and the trees about the nearby church were just budding.

'Are we paying for ourselves and having toasted tea cakes and tea as usual?' Lynn piped. 'I don't really expect you to pay.'

'It's my treat,' Julie insisted, giving her friend a quick affectionate glance.

'Great! Then get the letter out. Let me have a look-see.'

Julie dragged up her tote bag and then paused because the waitress had suddenly appeared. 'Tea and toasted buns. And a plate of cakes,' Julie ordered. Then she sat back to wait for the girl to go.

'Are you all right?' Lynn suddenly enquired, her bright eyes narrowed with concern.

'Of course I'm all right,' Julie assured. 'Here's the letter, Lynn. Read it carefully. Then you'll see what I'm up against.'

Lynn took the letter and sat back to read it while Julie turned to the window again.

She wasn't all right; something had happened to her. A great cloud of gloom had settled over her. And it had come down the moment she had set her eyes on the glamorous Dr Tulip driving off with the professor. She was jealous! She was falling for Eleven's surgeon.

You can't! You mustn't, something inside her warned. Don't make a fool of yourself. The Prof has something going with Dr Tulip. And by the glow on Susie's lovely face it's not an asexual relationship.

TWO

Eleven was in order again and no longer bore a resemblance to an emergency centre after a flood disaster. It was twenty to nine on the big round clock above the ward door and all was silent, the theatre cases happily sedated, the other patients thoughtfully silent. Staff Nurse Watson sat in the office, writing up the report while the auxiliary Simpson and Bella the ward maid gossiped in the kitchen. Julie glanced at the clock and then hurried into the kitchen to have a quick cup of tea with them.

The last of the supper dishes had been stacked away, the kitchen was tidy, and Bella, a stocky forty-year-old, with greying hair and gypsy dark eyes and all the cheek in the world, stood back against the sink to eye Julie. Poor kid, she thought, if she'd been my daughter she wouldn't have been slogging here. She hasn't the stamina. Or the nerve. Eleven was no lark for a sensitive youngster. All the same, she shouted, 'Mind you wash that pot out, Singer. I'm considerate but I'm not soft. And I've done my stint for the day.'

'Here come the night staff,' Simpson said. Julie drained her cup and then quickly washed it before stacking it away with the rest. 'Hurry up, Singer,' Simpson went on.

Yes, the night staff had arrived. Staff Nurse Watson was in the corridor, waiting for them. Julie hurried out of the kitchen after Simpson.

'You can go now, Nurses,' Staff Nurse Watson called cheerfully. 'Goodnight.'

'Goodnight, Staff.' Julie shot off along the annex before the homely auxiliary could waddle after her. She was in a hurry. She had to catch Lynn, insist that she did not write that report. She had made the decision; she would not take advantage of her friend's generosity, her impulsiveness. Her face flushed with anxiety, Julie almost broke out into a run, then, turning the corner at the end of the annex, she cried out as she crashed bodily into someone. He cursed softly and then gripped her arms to steady her.

Dark eyes stared angrily into Julie's blue. 'Nurse Singer! Is the ward on fire?'

The professor's tone was cool and controlled, only his dark eyes were stern with annoyance.

Fearfully, Julie stared back at him, then somehow she managed to gasp, 'I'm sorry, sir.' And had it not been for the hard hands which gripped her she felt her legs would have completely given way.

'Do you usually leave the ward at such a gallop?' he demanded, his eyes hard on her flushed face, her quivering lips.

Ridiculously, Julie heard herself stammer, 'I'm off duty, sir.'

Again their eyes met and held.

'I'm off duty also, Nurse,' he said evenly. 'But I don't intend to leave like a racing nag.'

'No, sir–I'm sorry, sir.' Julie twisted her arms free.

'Just a moment, Nurse.'

This time Adam Rich gripped Julie's shoulders and forced her to look at him. 'Is there something wrong?' he enquired. 'Can't you cope? You seem to have been in trouble all day.'

In his eyes, Julie saw not only a reprimand but also a faint gleam of interest; she knew that this surgeon was assessing not only her nursing conduct, but also something more personal. She also knew that she had blushed like some foolish schoolgirl. Again she struggled free. Desperately, she told him, 'I'm tired, I'm anxious to get to my room. That's all.'

'I see...' His narrowed eyes smiled cynically as he teased, 'I usually diagnose such behaviour as a broken affair... A disappointment. Perhaps...'

'Then your diagnosis is wrong, Professor,' Julie broke in furiously. 'I'd just had enough for one day–'

'Then I suggest you have a hot drink and an early night,' Adam Rich said, more gently and because he was conscious now of Julie's personal fragrance. 'You are worrying too much, Nurse. Relax.'

'Goodnight, sir,' Julie breathed.

And, watching her go, Adam Rich smiled for again Julie had gone off at breakneck speed.

Lynn was in her room. 'I've been waiting for you,' she said in an excited voice the moment Julie opened the door, 'I've got news. Your troubles are over. Read this. You could be nurse of the year. And what do you think of that for a forged signature?'

Julie kicked off her shoes and unpinned her cap. 'I've been thinking,' she said determinedly. 'And I don't want you to write that report, Lynn. It would really be criminal. I can't ask you to do such a thing.'

'It's done, darling. The vile deed is done. Go on, read it.'

Julie shook her head. 'No,' she insisted. 'I don't want to see it. Tear it up, Lynn. If you don't, I will.'

'Bloody hell!' Lynn cried. 'I've spent all afternoon concocting this gush.' Absently, she reached for the sheet of paper and slowly and deliberately she tore it up. 'There goes my dream,' she sighed. 'I'll be here until I begin to look like a sphygmomanometer. Do you know how many blood pressures I've taken today? Oh, Lord! And I thought you were going to get me off the hook. You know I'll never get my SRN.'

'I'm sorry, Lynn,' Julie sighed. 'I've had a rotten day on Eleven. And there was no junior on duty tonight. Just the auxiliary and myself. And Bella, of course! She kept us right.'

'Bloody ward maids are all the same. They're running the National Health Service.' Lynn laughed and then, glancing at her friend, 'You're not listening,' she accused.

'Sorry.' Julie laughed self-consciously. 'I almost managed to knock the Prof down as I left the ward. He thinks I'm an idiot.'

'You are!' Lynn emphasised. 'But never mind, we still want you to play for the concert the nurses are giving for the medics. It's in three weeks' time and I'm on the committee. I put your name forward.'

Astonished, Julie stared back at her friend. 'I didn't really want anyone to know that I played,' she stammered. 'I wish you hadn't mentioned me, Lynn.'

'Nonsense! Besides, I want to hear you play. I rather like classical music.'

'You might,' Julie breathed, 'but I'm sure the others don't. Oh, you know what they like. Get a punk group or something. The medics want fun, not culture. All those jostling students... All those prodding doctors! Oh, no...You'll have to forget about me.'

Lynn frowned. 'We really are in a fix,' she began more seriously. 'You would be doing us a favour, Julie. And, believe me, some of the medics do like the classical stuff. They're not all morons. Please, Julie ... I'm going to look such a fool if you won't.' A long look and then Lynn went on slyly, 'The Prof is dead keen on the Proms. He'll listen even if no one else does. So here is your chance. You don't really want him to think you're an idiot, do you?'

'How do you know he likes music?' Julie began carefully.

'Because he asked Sister to get him two tickets for an organ recital at the cathedral. I also saw her hand them over. He looked very pleased.'

Lynn considered her friend for a moment, then said, 'Well, do you want to prove that you're no dumbo? Here is your chance. And I would be grateful, Julie... We haven't got much going for us, so far.'

'Oh, all right,' Julie laughed. 'I'll play. And if you'll remove your sexy body from my bed I think I'll have an early night.'

'Sexy body! If I don't have any luck soon I may as well give it to research.' Lynn's eyes suddenly sparkled. 'However, I'll not be impulsive; there is a smashing physio-therapist I've got my eyes on. He might just

42

be a good manipulator!'

'I wish you'd stop playing and do a bit of swotting,' Julie complained. 'If you don't stop chasing the fellows, you'll get a name for yourself.'

'Better than going unnoticed, lamb.' Lynn suddenly sprang up. 'Joking apart,' she said, assuming a more sober expression, 'I'll inform the committee. We're not doing too badly,' she added with another grin. 'We've got you and that stuffy looking nurse on ENT. She rings handbells.'

'If you are off tomorrow afternoon we could go down to town,' Julie called after her. 'I'd like a look round the shopping complex. I might even buy something.'

'I know. A dress for the concert?'

'Perhaps.'

'Good ... you've got the right idea.'

'Hang on a tick, Lynn,' Julie called.

'How the devil could I do that,' Lynn joked. 'What is it?'

'Your do-it-yourself revision, dear. It might do you some good if you kept it in your own room.'

Lynn pulled a face and then closed the door after her. Julie undressed quickly and slipped on her dressing-gown. For a few moments she gazed gravely back at her reflection in the long wardrobe mirror. So at last she was going to play to an audience of sorts. The idea excited her a little and, smiling wistfully now, she turned to the door. She was out of practice, she realised, but the concert was not for another three weeks, so she had time to limber up. She also had time to change her mind, she reminded herself. But, no, she decided, as she ran her bath, that would be mean, churlish. But she had problems.

Julie lay back in the warm, scented water to consider these problems. She would definitely hear from the solicitors again. Or perhaps they would write to her parent. She felt they would not go over her head and communicate directly with Matron. No, she still had time to make plans, to think. Perhaps she should drop them a line, to say that Matron was on holiday.

Soaping herself again, Julie now thought of the concert. And she smiled at the idea of astonishing the Professor, proving she was no dumbo, as Lynn had put it. Yes, it would give her some satisfaction to show him what she could do with a keyboard. Trained, she might even have learnt to wield a scalpel, but making music, that took talent. A gift, her mother called it.

Later, in bed, Julie thought of her mother and her young brother. She loved them so much, she could not let them down. She would not. Somehow she would get her SRN, then pick up the legacy and, after settling the family she would return to her music. Julie closed her eyes as a familiar rippling stream of notes filled her brain... She loved Chopin... One of the masters had told her she had a unique style of interpretation of his work...

Julie sighed in her sleep and then,

'Six o'clock, Nurse!'

A door on Virgins' Alley slammed shut

and instantly Julie was awake and contemplating yet another day on Eleven. Springing out of bed, she quickly washed. Then, after slipping on her uniform, she hurried out into the corridor. Lynn was locking her own front door further up as Julie called, yawningly, 'Morning, Lynn...' and then waited for her friend to fall in step beside her.

'I've been awake half the night thinking about that report for your solicitors,' Lynn grumbled. 'Now, if I'd been you, I'd have had it written and off. You must be crazy, Julie... All that money!'

In the lift, crammed with early risers, they fell silent but the moment they started through the conservatory Julie said, 'I've decided to make them wait, Lynn. Bluff my way for a while. If I don't answer their letter they'll possibly think I didn't receive it and write again. It will all take time, and that's what I'm playing for at the moment.'

'My offer still holds,' Lynn sang out as life surged back into her veins. 'On a percentage basis, of course,' she laughed.

Through the swing doors and at once all the sounds and smells of the hospital were all about them; lifts whirred, trolleys rattled, nurses rustled by and from the ward at the far end of the long corridor came the cries of the babies just awakened.

Julie and Lynn walked on quickly towards the Dining Room, then Lynn asked, 'Are you going to play for us, Julie? I'll have to let the committee know.'

'Oh, yes, I'll play,' Julie answered casually. 'I'll have to put in some practice, and that won't do me any harm.'

'Great! That's super!' Pleased, Lynn forged ahead and into the Dining Room, where she quickly found a table for herself and Julie. 'If it's fish again I'll go berserk,' she said under her breath. 'Fish and their cakes, that's all our dieticians seems to think about.'

'I'm just having toast,' Julie said as she sat down. 'I never have time to get through their haddock.'

Lynn smirked. 'I'll have to eat something,' she said, and she marched off to help herself. 'Sure I can't get you some?' she called back.

'Positive.'

As usual, they ate their breakfast in comparative silence, but when they had finished, Lynn asked, 'Are you off this morning, Julie?'

Julie nodded.

'See you tonight, then.' Lynn scraped back her chair. 'I'm not off until six.'

A few moments later Julie followed a group of nurses making for the door and their respective wards, and as she made her way towards Eleven she wondered what the day had in store for her. It was the early morning hospital routine that she hated most, the abrupt start which began the moment the night nurse rapped on her door. The discipline!

Glancing down the ward, Julie was surprised to see the houseman already on the ward and then, making her way down the annex, she was suddenly aware of a peculiar silence. Passing the Day Room door, she glanced in and stiffened a little when she saw the daughter of one of the patients, sitting very straight and still on one of the chairs.

And then a commotion on the corridor jerked Julie to attention and, to her amazement, she saw Professor Rich accompanied by David Whittaker and the Night Staff Nurse coming towards her.

Had Mrs Stone died? She had had major surgery. Julie felt a wave of panic sweep through her. As yet, she had never been asked to help with the last offices for anyone. She prayed that Mrs Stone would not die until she had gone off duty. Then, flushed with the shame of her own cowardly, selfish thoughts, Julie stood back against the cold tiled wall of the annex to allow the small group to pass. And just for a fraction of a second, dark eyes held her own. But this time the Professor's gaze had been indifferent; without interest. He had not recognised her, Julie told herself, then she hurried on towards the ward.

'Nurse Singer!'

'Yes, Sister. Reporting for duty.'

'Mrs Stone, the hysterectomy hae-morrhaged,' Sister Grey told Julie swiftly. 'She's on a drip now. The Professor has just seen her. You had better make beds with the junior. Then start temps. I'll read the report later.'

'Yes, Sister.' Relieved to know that Mrs Stone was still alive, Julie rushed off to find the junior, who was giving the night junior a hand with the laundry in the Sluice Room.

'They've had a shocking night,' Nurse Dixon whined the moment she saw Julie. 'I'm just helping Nurse with these sheets.'

'You've got to make beds with me,' Julie said evenly. 'Come on, Dixon. We'll have to get a move on ourselves.'

The scraggy Nurse Dixon was a gossip. As they stripped the first bed she began, 'They certainly didn't get any shut-eye last night. And Whittaker had to call the Prof in the end. Her veins had collapsed or something. Mrs Stone! And that awful daughter of hers is stuck in the Day Room. I expect they had to drag her out of bed, like the Gestapo. She couldn't care less about her mother. She never visits.'

'Nurse,' Julie reprimanded gravely, 'would you see to that corner. Keep your mind on your work. Sister's not going to be in too good a mood today. And let's give Mrs Dobson a lift up the bed. She'll be more comfortable.'

Mrs Dobson, a soulful sort, raised pained eyes and then sank back against her pillows. 'That's better,' she sighed. 'It's the little things that count, you know...'

Together, they passed on to the next bed where a cheerful-looking round-faced woman sat. 'Shall I jump out?' she asked.

'Please...' Julie gave the woman a smile.

'As long as you don't get your tubes in a twist,' Dixon teased.

'Cheeky...' the woman flung back, but she was still smiling.

The young Dixon was very confident.

The bed empty, they were able to make it up at the speed of light. Dixon prattled on to the patient but Julie's thoughts began to stray. Adam Rich had looked tired, and preoccupied. Perhaps he had not recognised her? But the curtain screen had been removed from Mrs Stone's bed; the patient was still with them. Julie glanced across the ward at the woman it seemed Adam Rich had just recalled to life and suddenly she felt a rush of pride. She was proud to work with such people, proud even of the red-headed rugby-playing Whittaker.

'A penny for your thoughts, Nurse Singer,' the patient said as she climbed back into bed. 'You're very quiet this morning, Nurse.'

'Breakfast was lousy,' Julie said, and pulled a face before walking on to the next bed.

After the bed-making was over, Julie took the temps and then set out the flowers.

And now the rest of the morning was to be her own!

Making her way back to her room, Julie bumped into Lynn, who was just going for coffee before going back to her ward. Excitedly, Lynn told her, 'You know that stodgy bird on Skins? The one who rings handbells. We've got her. And Angela on Orthopaedic is getting a group together.'

Glancing at the rain that beat on the conservatory glass, Julie said, 'I may even spend the morning at the piano...'

'You do that. See you tonight, Julie.'

Because she had decided not to go out, Julie did not bother to change into mufti. She went straight to the Nurses' Sitting Room and, finding it deserted, she quickly closed the door. It was almost six months since she had last touched a keyboard. And now, with a kind of reverence, she approached the grand piano. She sat down, and then drew her fingers over the keys. And in that fraction of time, with this simple gesture, Julie felt her whole being expand with joy.

This was her world, this was her love. For

her music she had all the drive in the world. In her mind's eye now she acknowledged the conductor, the house lights dimmed, she raised her hands. And with an incredible expertise for one so young Julie played Beethoven's Third Piano Concerto to the accompaniment of an orchestra which she alone could hear. The Third was her first love, and now as she played tingles of sheer joy ran up her spine, her skin gleamed, her blue eyes grew moist. Greater than any love was her love for music.

Julie played not only with technical skill but with emotion. And now she offered her gift to another, one whose skill she felt surpassed her own. For even now she could not dismiss Adam from her mind. Everything beautiful, everything harmonious she offered up to him. It was her symphony for a surgeon.

A voice raised in amazement brought Julie back to reality. Abruptly, she stopped playing. The spell was broken. It was one of the nurses from the Casualty Hall but she did not know her name.

'You're good,' the girl cried, peering more closely at Julie, as though she had found some odd species. 'I love the Third. Mind, I don't suppose any of the morons here would recognise it... Go on. Don't let me disturb you.'

'The mood just caught me,' Julie said, standing up, glancing at another nurse who had just come into the room.

'I really must get down to gall bladders,' the slim blonde from Men's Surgical said with a titter. 'Anyone like to help.'

As the blonde threw down her textbook, Julie quickly made for the door and then her own room. After a session with her music it was agonisingly painful to find herself back in such an alien scene. Gall bladders! Ulcers! A sudden desperation gripped her and, without realising it, Julie locked her door before flinging herself down on her bed. She had forgotten nothing; the Third had just fallen from her fingertips. And now all she wanted to do was sit at a piano, get on with what destiny had ordained. She was a concert pianist. How could she ever be a nurse!

★ ★ ★ ★

Three weeks later, Julie went down into town and bought herself a new long cotton skirt and a blouse. Just prowling round the boutique, which reminded her of Aladdin's cave, made her feel brighter, happier. The skirt was gay, splashed with flowers and sprigs of greenery, the blouse a little more stylish and in silk. And most suitable for the concert. She was hanging them up when the door opened and Lynn popped her head round the door.

'Oh, you're back,' Lynn said, stepping into the room. 'What did you get?'

'I'll show you tonight,' Julie said brightly. 'I'm off at six, so I'll have plenty of time to get ready.'

'You're not going to get nerves or anything?' Lynn said, her eyes hard on Julie.

'I've backed you two to one, darling. I reckon you're a winner. The punk rockers first and then you. You can't fail to be a sensation.'

'I'll try not to let you down,' Julie said from beneath her uniform dress, which she was pulling over her head.

'I won't keep you,' Lynn said, her hand on the door again. 'But have you heard anything from the solicitors? I'm an interested party, if nothing else.'

Julie shook her head. 'Not yet,' she called, as she fastened on her cap. 'So I'm okay for the time being. I'm certainly not thinking of them at the moment.'

'See you tonight, then.'

The door closed after Lynn, and Julie smiled to herself. Already she felt elated, alive, her head full of fresh harmonies, new combinations of sound. And tonight she was to play to an audience.

For the first time in months she felt happy.

All afternoon Julie packed sterilising drums on Eleven. It was visiting day and

Sister Grey was off duty, and for once Staff Nurse Watson seemed to be taking it easy. They had no seriously ill patients and even the visitors looked relaxed. Sunlight streamed through the ward windows and as Julie worked she thought of Adam Rich. Would he, she wondered, be at the concert?

★ ★ ★ ★

The concert hall was packed; every seat taken, the walls lined with nurses and students, the front stalls taken by consultants, registrars and surgeons. There was an air of excitement, frivolity. The show had begun; a bevy of nurses from the Skin Department were dancing a riotous can-can. The dance grew wilder and wilder, the shouts and whistles louder and louder. The show had got off to a good start.

Next came the sexy, dark-haired staff nurse from Men's Surgical. Wrapped in a ward teacloth and nothing else she sang in a sexy, sultry manner, which made the medics titter and the quick-snip surgeon who did the vasectomies look even more lethal.

And then the punk rockers from Out-Patients. One of the nurses had dyed her hair a coral pink and she wore an almost see-through mac. A fat one wore winkle-pickers and a black plastic shirt and another one had a ring through her nose. They sang a song out of key and got banned by Matron before they had reached the third verse.

Watching from the wings, Julie rolled her eyes at Lynn. 'I'm suddenly terrified,' she whispered tremulously. 'I could run away.'

'Oh, they're more cultured than they look,' said Lynn, who looked more like an ostrich than a ballet dancer. 'You'll be O.K Julie. Think of me. I'll probably get a bucket of water over me and go off like a sodden cockerel.'

Julie had to smile. As the leader of the corps de ballet, Lynn did look ridiculous; her legs were too long, her feet too big.

'Listen,' hissed Lynn again, 'there's Sister from Casualty giving you a big build-up. It's you, kid Go on.'

Taking a deep breath, Julie then made her way on to the stage and, after a quick, shy acknowledgement of her audience, she took her seat at the piano. The house lights dimmed. In her mind's eye, Julie saw the conductor raise his baton.

And now with great expertise she played Beethoven's Third, her favourite concerto. The *Allegro con brio* held her audience rapt, the most mischievous eyes grew soulful, the most austere softened with admiration.

She was holding them!

Julie smiled as she played now, carried away by the melodious theme she knew so well. Confidently, she broke into the second movement, and then unknown to Julie the swing doors at the back of the hall opened and a very odd figure, stepped out on to the middle aisle. A figure which gradually drew everyone's attention and invoked a titter of humour from those nearby who recognised the practical joker as he came down the aisle on slippered knees, wearing a top hat and bow-tie and carrying a cane and looking for all the world like the dwarfed figure of the artist Toulouse-Lautrec.

The titter grew and, conscious now that something was wrong, Julie glanced swiftly at her audience. She saw the dwarf and her heart leapt up, her fingers stumbled. The spell was broken. Broken by a student with a soul like a suet dumpling. Everyone was laughing now, the nurses self-consciously, the students gaffawing and calling, 'Bring on the girls! Bring on the can-can dancers!'

Julie caught a glimpse of one or two outraged faces, then with a rush of both embarrassment and fury, she shakily stood up and made her way off the stage. Never, never in all her life had she felt so foolish! So humiliated!

'That bastard!' Lynn raged. 'He's one of our lot. I'll give him hell in the morning.' As Lynn started on to the stage she managed to call, 'Honestly, Julie, you were marvellous...'

Julie had vanished. Another uproar broke out in the hall. In dismay, Julie looked about her, then dizzily she made her way back to the Nurse's Home. She felt as though a sandstorm had blown up in her brain; fury blinded her. She should have known better than to let anyone persuade her to play to the medics. Everyone knew how uncultured they were. Oh, God! She felt so awful. So ridiculous! If only she could run away? She didn't even want to be a nurse!

As Julie rushed madly along the main corridor, tears of anger streamed down her face. She reached the conservatory and then, just as she was about to push through the swing doors, a hard, purposeful hand came down on her shoulder.

'Nurse Singer!'

Julie spun round.

'I had a job to keep up with you,' Adam Rich said in a quiet, controlled voice. 'I had to congratulate you.'

'Congratulate me?' Julie's young voice rang with cynical anger. Dismay made her turn from him.

'If those tears are from rage, then carry

on,' he said gently, his fingers turning about Julie's arm now. 'I do understand. I also understand my students. They'll give that practical joker hell in the morning. At the moment they're carried away by something like hysteria. They're working hard at being hilarious.'

'I felt so terrible,' Julie confessed weakly. 'So silly.'

'Why? You played superbly, Nurse. That's why I came hotfoot after you. I had to congratulate you. You may keep the surgeons waiting, but, my God, Nurse, you are a talented girl. I am quite willing to forgive all your other discrepancies.'

He was smiling, his eyes were steady with a tender concern. Julie felt her pulse quicken. 'They're nothing but a mob of baboons,' she suddenly burst out. 'I've never met such people.'

'Look, Nurse ... will you come out and have a drink with me?'

His suggestion made Julie's heart leap up. She stared at him.

'It might help. And believe me, I appreciated that performance. The Third is one of my favourite concertos. I can't tell you how I felt when I heard you playing it. I was astounded.' Slipping his arm about her shoulder, he coaxed, 'Come on. A drive and a drink and Nurse Singer will be herself again.'

For a while the atmosphere in the car was heavy with embarrassment. Julie constantly cleared her throat; again and again she tried to think of something suitable to say to a surgeon. Then, to her relief, Adam began to chat. He talked non-stop all the way to the coast, which was ten miles distance from the hospital. He certainly knew something about music, Julie thought as he parked their car in the forecourt of a small hotel by the sea.

'Feeling better?' he enquired and momentarily his hand touched Julie's.

She nodded. 'I'll get over it,' she laughed shakily. 'Though it was a little disconcerting. I felt such a fool.' Feeling a little more at ease, she added jokingly, 'I just hope you haven't missed anything really good.'

Opening the car door, Adam then took Julie's hand and drew her towards the entrance. 'You know,' he said, pausing to give her a long look, 'it had occurred to me that you would do better on another ward. Now I've changed my mind. I intend to keep my eye on you, Nurse Singer. Setting aside douche lotions and major surgery, I think we may yet have something in common.'

'You mean I may not be an idiot after all,' Julie rebuked and this time she raised her eyebrows.

'I never thought you were an idiot!' Now Adam's hand closed more firmly over Julie's and again she was conscious of her wild, palpitating heart. It was like a dream. To walk at Adam Rich's side pleased her more than any thundering applause. She gave him another smile and then together they wandered into the lounge bar, where Adam found a table for them by the window. And while he ordered drinks, Julie turned to the sea, which was just beginning to merge with the sky. Soon it would be dark.

Over their drinks Julie talked about music and very soon her awkwardness vanished. Adam sat back, his legs outstretched before him, an expression of intense interest in his dark eyes.

'What the devil are you doing at St George's?' he exclaimed at last, leaning forward a little to study Julie's flushed face. 'My girl, I think you have a gift.'

'Nonsense,' Julie returned, her hand steadying on her glass. 'I just enjoy music.'

'I enjoy it too ... but compared with you, I don't know a thing about it. Nor can I play an instrument. Nurse Singer,' he began, then he suddenly frowned and sat back abruptly to stare at Julie. 'I can't call you Nurse,' he exclaimed, a baffled look coming into his eyes. 'What is your name?'

'Julie – Julie Singer.'

'Julie – Julie Singer.' Savouring the name,

he continued to stare at Julie, then he smiled again and told her, 'All right, Julie, I take my hat off to you. You continue to astonish me.'

'Continue to?' Julie shook out her hair with an involuntary gesture, opened her blue eyes wide.

'Well,' he grinned, 'I had noticed your very blue eyes. I suppose they've kept you out of a bit of trouble?' He laughed again, as though at himself this time.

'I want more than anything else to be a good nurse,' she told him deliberately. 'I admire the nurses. I admire and respect everyone who works in a hospital.'

'Do you admire me?' he asked.

A teasing smile on his lips, and Julie flushed up. 'I admire the work you do,' she told him. 'You have a very special gift, Professor Rich. Where there is despair, you bring hope–'

'Thank you, Julie.' Adam Rich leaned forward now, his eyes narrowed curiously as he studied Julie's grave young face. 'I won't forget those words. But let me say that the musician also has an important role. Where there is discord the musician brings harmony.' Straightening up again, he frowned a little and added less seriously, 'Perhaps you would be willing to call me Adam ... when we happen to be off duty.'

It was dark when they left the lounge and, as they made their way back to the car, Adam slid a protective arm about Julie's shoulders. 'This way,' he murmured. Reaching the car, he opened the door for Julie and then stood back to stand silently for a few moments, watching the lights of a ship far out at sea. Then, glancing at Julie again, he said in a low-pitched voice, 'Perhaps we'll not be too hard on that practical joker. I enjoyed that drink, Julie. Did you?'

'Very much,' Julie answered, feeling awkward again.

THREE

'For Pete's sake!' Lynn said. 'Snap out of it, Julie. You've been in the doldrums for a week. And take my advice, unless you need your tubes blown or unravelled, keep out of the way of the Prof. He's not the bloke for you, Julie. He's too old for a start.'

'Oh, shut up, Lynn,' Julie defended herself. 'You don't know what you're talking about.'

'I know the old boy felt sorry for you,' Lynn went on. 'But I felt sorry for you! It was a rotten thing to happen. And I can tell you this, that practical joker isn't enjoying life any more.'

'Another one you had an affair with?' Julie accused.

'Hardly,' Lynn interjected. 'That idiot is about as intelligent as my big toe.'

69

Her voice small and sober, Julie said, 'Adam has a sensitive soul. And he is not old, Lynn.'

'Perhaps not that old, but there is also Susie. And, my God, Susie is as sensitive as sandpaper when it comes to the Prof. Take my advice and forget him, Julie.' Lynn spoke feelingly but she knew Julie was barely listening.

'Was Susie Tulip at the concert?' Julie enquired after a few moments.

'Of course not!' Lynn battled on. 'She was on call. Do you think the Prof would have leapt up to your defence if Susie had been with him? And, please, Julie, don't call the Prof Adam ... it kind of makes me nervous.'

Julie continued to tidy her dressing-table. Plagued by confusion, tortured by jealousy, she could not keep still. Lynn urged her to forget the Prof. But she could not. Night and day Adam Rich was there in her mind, urging her on to more intimate and dangerous ideas. He had called her 'Julie'. They were friends! She called him 'Adam'.

And she was already in love with him.

'Have you heard from those solicitors?' Lynn asked gravely, her eyes hard on Julie.

'I heard this morning,' Julie said. 'They're getting impatient.'

'So am I,' Lynn returned snappily. 'It's ridiculous. All you've got to do is send my letter. I have a copy and the offer still holds.' With a grin, she added slyly, 'Though at one per cent higher. I have no future, you know. I'm just here for the dirty work and to give everyone a laugh. I'll never even pass an exam. I'm too much of a clown.'

For a moment Julie forgot her own problems and, staring at her friend, she thought with a rush of compassion, she's speaking the truth, she'll never pass an exam. All the same, she knew that Lynn was worth her weight in gold on the ward. The patients loved her, the nurses suffered her, happily. 'Do you really want to be a nurse, Lynn?' she asked carefully.

'Of course I do,' Lynn asserted. 'I love the work. Besides,' she giggled, 'what else could

I do. I just wish I could tickle the ivories.'

That was just like Lynn. 'I don't tickle the ivories,' Julie suddenly snapped, her anger roused. 'I happen to have been training to be a concert pianist since I was ten years old, Lynn.'

'Okay ... okay. I know. Keep your cool, Julie. It must be hard for you. But it's hard for me thinking about all that lovely loll...'

'Yes,' Julie sighed. 'I've just got to get my SRN and it's mine. And then I'll be able to return to my own wonderful world of music. I don't fit in here, Lynn. I feel so alien – so utterly lost, miserable at times.'

'But not with the Prof?' Lynn taunted. 'And he uses surgical spirit for after-shave.'

'Oh, you are crazy,' Julie flung. 'I feel excited by him because he understands music. He knows it, he loves it, I feel he does ... I can see he does.'

'I must go,' Lynn said, suddenly tiring. 'I may just pick up a textbook this afternoon. But I mean what I say, Julie – you sign for that legacy and you'll soon forget the Prof. I wouldn't even chance an affair with that demon barber. But, never mind, I must go. God bless your heart. And all your other vital organs, of course.'

'Pick up that do-it-yourself surgery,' Julie reminded. 'I'm going to get changed and then have a wander down town.'

'See you...' Lynn called as she picked up the book and made for the door.

The moment the door closed, Julie returned to the window ledge, where she sat absently watching the players on the court below. Definitely now, she did not want to leave St George's. But for another reason. She wanted to be near Adam. Something told her that they would meet again. She smiled secretly as she listened to the voices which drifted pleasantly up to her. Susie Tulip was gorgeous; beautiful and clever. A woman with the right background for a man like Adam Rich. But Susie did not hold all the cards...

Suddenly Julie wanted to buy some exciting new make-up, something that would bring her into full focus. She wanted to be noticed. No longer was she content to be there, or not there – like a fawn in a sunlit glade.

★ ★ ★ ★

Ward Eleven was no sunlit glade.

'You'd better do the treatment and dressings, Nurse,' Sister Grey said, her eyes disapprovingly on Julie's new vibrant lipstick. 'Nurse Baron has her preps to get on with.'

'I could do with a gin and penicillin,' Baron the theatre nurse said as she passed Julie on the ward. 'I've got a bit of a throat.'

'Ask Sister for something,' Julie suggested absently, then, turning round, she headed back down the annex corridor to the Sterilising Room, where the dressing trolley stood in readiness. She peered at the list of dressings to be done, then turned on the steriliser. There was no time to waste on Eleven.

Half an hour later, as Julie was turning down the clothes at bed thirteen, she heard a sound of footsteps on the corridor and, peering round the bed screens, she saw Professor Rich and his entourage heading for the ward.

At once Julie felt the colour flooding up from her throat to her face. 'It's the Prof,' she gasped.

'Professor Rich!' It was the turn of the woman in the bed to turn now. 'Will he be coming to see me?'

'I don't know.' Julie's hand shook as she quickly turned up the bedclothes again. 'But don't worry,' she encouraged. 'He'll see that we're busy.'

'It sounds as though his merry men are with him,' the woman said, her eyes rolling with anxiety.

'There's no need to panic,' Julie said under her breath. 'We all suffer from that mob. Anyhow, you are respectable.'

'Thank God for that!' The patient sighed again, and then smiled at Julie.

But even then Julie knew that the Prof and his jostling medical students, Sister Grey and Whittaker the houseman, had already stopped at the other side of the screen.

The curtain swung back.

'Good evening, Nurse,' the Prof said in a controlled tone, but his smile was for the patient. 'And how are you, Mrs Jenkins?' he enquired. 'Comfortable?'

At a loss for words, Mrs Jenkins exchanged a glance with Julie. In the background one of the students tittered.

'Well, we'll not keep you from your work, Nurse.' This time the Prof gave Julie a quick smile. 'But just for the benefit of my students you would perhaps tell them what percentage lotion you are using for Mrs Jenkins' douche?'

Douche? What percentage? Julie's thoughts ricocheted round her head. Suddenly she could not capture one of them. Numbly she stared back at the Prof. Again, somewhere in the background someone tittered.

'Nurse Singer!' Sister Grey spoke up sharply. 'You surely know what you're doing?'

'Yes, yes, I do, Sister. I just cannot remember the percentage.' Julie stammered.

'You will, Nurse.' The Prof's voice broke in with a cool arrogance. 'Unless of course you are tired? Or bored? Or not even interested?'

The entourage moved on. Julie heard the curtain swish round the rails again. She stared at her patient.

'Don't let it upset you,' Mrs Jenkins said under her breath and reaching to pat Julie's hand. 'These clever people are often unkind. If you'd just looked at me I could have told you. I've seen it on the bottle often enough. It's lactic acid, one half per cent, isn't it?'

With chagrin, Julie stared back at Mrs Jenkins, then with a frown she said, 'My head went numb. Some people have that effect on me. But you have nothing to fear, Mrs Jenkins. Everything is checked twice.

Like the medicines.'

With a smile, Julie's patient lay back against her pillows and Julie drew down the sheet again. 'You would have made a good nurse,' she said in a tone of appraisal.

The woman smiled back. 'And you are a good nurse,' she said with emphasis. 'Some people just have a way of emptying your head. I remember one man I knew ... every time I saw him, I forgot my own name.' Laughing at this reflection, Mrs Jenkins again patted Julie's hand and advised in a motherly tone, 'Take things as they come, Nurse. Don't get so uptight. Watch Nurse Baron. See how cool she keeps.'

Half an hour later David Whittaker came breezing down the ward. 'No one escaped,' he called. 'Something must have really upset the Prof. Wow! There's something different. New lipstick?'

Julie smiled at last.

'Keep it,' the red-headed houseman grinned. 'It suits you.' And after a whistle. 'Makes those eyes look even more blue. You could well have knocked the old boy off course.'

'Are you looking for someone?' Julie enquired as casually as she could manage.

'Yes.' Whittaker glanced at the case-sheet in his hand. 'Hilda Pottermus.' His gaze went to the enormous woman propped up in one of the beds at the bottom of the ward. 'Before we can do anything with Mrs Potter she must lose four stone. I've told Sister to put her on to a thousand calories a day. With knuckles like a navvy and a fifty-inch bust – how did she ever arrive on *ELEVEN?*'

Julie pushed her trolley forward as she mumbled, 'The Prof didn't stay very long.'

'He just wanted to see his new patient. The ruptured ectopic he did yesterday,' Whittaker informed. 'She's fine.' Moving on, Whittaker called back, 'He's having coffee with Sister now.'

Julie continued with the dressings and at seven o'clock Sister's door opened and the Prof strode off down the annex. Sister Grey came into the ward, smiling and looking less like a brigadier than usual.

'If you've finished the dressings, Nurse Singer,' she called in an offhand fashion, 'there's some coffee left in the pot.'

Julie stared after her. So Sister Grey had a heart, she could be quite human. She had expected to be blown sky high over the lactic acid incident. She had, after all, stood there looking quite witless. And she certainly would appreciate a coffee.

The coffee was hot and Sister Grey's generosity did much to restore Julie's confidence and the rest of the evening on Eleven went without any further trouble.

As she walked back to the Nurses' Home Julie's head began to fill with the music she loved so well, and by the time she reached the post office she was far away in a safe and familiar world of her own. It was Sister Cole who broke the spell.

'Nurse Singer!' she called sharply. 'A letter for you.'

'A letter! Oh, thanks.' Julie's voice shook as she took the letter and then proceeded quickly to the lift. And as the lift whirred up to the first floor she glanced at the handwriting. It was not from the solicitors. And it was not from her mother. In fact, she did not recognise the writing.

Once in her room, Julie wasted no time in opening the envelope. Frowningly, she began to read it. And then, suddenly, her cheeks were aflame.

Dear Julie,

I am entertaining a small party of friends at my home next Friday evening and I wondered if you would be prepared to come and entertain us. I would consider this a great favour and would look forward immensely to hearing you play again.

Hoping to hear from you soon ... and trusting that the coffee was still hot.

Yours,

ADAM RICH

Julie fell back against the cool wall of her bedroom. Her heart beat wildly. So Adam had felt as miserable as she had done herself. He had asked Sister to leave her that coffee. That was why Sister Grey had avoided looking at her! And now he had invited her to his home, to meet his friends. His letter had come as an assurance, a reminder that she was not just a nurse, but a musician. A reminder that he appreciated the fact that she could play the Third Piano Concerto even if she was a bit witless where percentages of lotion were concerned. With a rush of emotion, Julie sank down on to the side of the small bed. Oh, yes, she would play for Adam's guests, she thought ecstatically. It would be wonderful to go to his party, to be accepted as one of his friends. It would be wonderful to play for Adam. Every note, she thought with a rush of emotion, would surely be a declaration of her love.

The following Friday morning another note came in reply to Julie's. It was brief, merely intimating that a taxi would pick her up that evening at seven o'clock.

It was in a state of elation that Julie

dressed for the party. She had decided to wear a cotton skirt and a gypsy blouse. After spending some time making up her eyes, Julie at last slipped on her skirt and then turned to her long wardrobe mirror. She saw a slim, grave-eyed girl with soft brown hair. An ordinary girl, she thought with a rush of apprehension and saw in her mind's eye the gorgeous blonde Susie Tulip. Another quick gloss over her lips, and Julie decided that she had done her utmost to look attractive. She picked up a triangular shawl, her handbag and then quickly made her way out on to Virgins' Alley and to the lift.

The taxi arrived promptly and within ten minutes it was on the outskirts of the city and pulling up outside a large Victorian house from the windows of which lights blazed. A striking-looking woman, who introduced herself as Adam's sister, welcomed Julie to the party.

'So you are the little nurse Adam was telling us all about,' she said in a low, musical voice. 'Come in, my dear. Let me take your shawl. I'm so pleased you were able to come. We're all such music lovers in this house. Now, just a moment, dear, I must tell Adam that you have arrived.'

Nervously, Julie stared round, at the stained-glass front door, the panelled mirrors and dark leather settee. A Victorian plant-stand drew her attention. She could hear the sound of music coming from an inner room, the sound of raised voices, laughter. And suddenly Julie felt afraid; afraid of Adam's clever friends, friends who belonged to his own world.

And why had she been asked to wait?

Julie's heart began to beat very fast, she glanced at the door again when a deep masculine voice said,

'Oh, there you are, Julie...'

Julie's eyes met his and at once she thought, he looks fantastic. Tall with broad shoulders, a romantic figure in his deep black velvet jacket, open-necked shirt and gay silk scarf. Younger too, far removed from the white-coated surgeon with stern eyes and no time for careless nurses. Julie glanced away, as though afraid of what he might read in her eyes. 'Well,' she said a little breathlessly, 'I'm here. What would you like me to play?' Because he did not answer her at once, she flicked him another look, and suddenly his dark eyes were so gentle that she thought she might burst into tears.

'Thank you for coming, Julie,' he said in a low voice, his eyes still hard on the girl he knew to be suffering agonies of shyness, and whom he was more used to seeing pumping a sphygmomanometer or making a bed. Taking her hand firmly, he said, 'Play what you wish, but first of all I would like to introduce you to my friends. They're a noisy lot and they drink too much but I'm sure they are all going to be agreeably surprised.'

As he pushed open the double doors which led into a large sitting-room, he suggested, 'Perhaps you would play for us before dinner? That would give us all a pleasant topic of conversation. Certainly a change from the usual peptic ulcers. Or shall we keep them waiting?'

'Oh, there you are, darling!'

At that moment, Dr Tulip came forward to take Adam's arm possessively. She glanced up at Adam and then frowned a little in puzzlement.

'This is Nurse Julie Singer,' Adam introduced in a raised voice, 'and Julie has kindly offered to play for us.'

Heads nodded, glasses were raised. 'Good evening,' this one and that one called. 'Come and have a drink,' another vaguely familiar voice insisted.

Susie Tulip said, 'Of course! You're on Eleven, aren't you, Nurse?'

Julie nodded.

'Then welcome,' she sang out, and Julie guessed that Susie had already drunk a little too much.

Julie glanced at Adam again and for some reason he took her hand and squeezed it encouragingly. 'I'll get you a drink,' he told her. 'Just a small one. Any preference?'

Julie shook her head. 'A small sherry,' she told him, then to her surprise she saw David Whittaker, their houseman, coming straight towards her.

'Fancy seeing you,' he grinned. And as Adam Rich moved away, he teased in an undertone, 'You should be ashamed of yourself. The man's twice your age. But, never mind, just look out for Susie.'

Julie glanced away and at that moment she saw Susie Tulip regarding her with eyes which were plainly hostile. Then she recognised one of St George's paediatricians and she gave him a quick, shy smile.

Adam returned with her drink and, feeling very self-conscious, nervously sipping her sherry, Julie suddenly told him, 'This is nice and I must say I'm glad of it. As glad as I was of that coffee you told Sister to leave me, Adam. What a dim-wit you must take me for.'

'Not at all.' As he spoke his arm slid about Julie's back in a warm, comforting gesture. 'But no shop talk tonight, Julie,' he went on softly. 'You must, though, keep on calling me Adam. I like it. And it suits you. Also it makes me feel less old.'

'You can't be *that* old!' Julie half teased, half defended. 'I mean you do still wield a scalpel.' In the back of her mind she was still wondering what he had meant by 'it suits you'. 'I just find you so intimidating,' she confessed girlishly. 'I knew the percentage of that lotion. You make me forget.'

'I do?' He gave her another long look, then suddenly he was smiling, and removing his arm, and saying rather throatily, 'I suppose we shouldn't let the guests get too hungry. What about playing for us now, Julie?'

'Just as you wish,' Julie answered, yet still feeling far from relaxed. 'I just hope they're in the mood for classical music.' As she spoke her gaze went round the room, and it was not to confidently. Someone was re-arranging the furniture, another adjusting the lighting. Susie Tulip, a little tight, was trying to get a middle-aged heart specialist to dance with her. Whittaker was at the bar, eyeing a woman who would have looked better in a cloak and mask.

The doorbell was ringing furiously again. Someone else had arrived.

And there were knots in Julie's stomach.

'What will you play?'

'Fantaisie Impromptu,' Julie whispered. 'It's not too long.' Glancing again at her audience, she added ruefully, 'And if I haven't to make a quick get-away, then perhaps, a Chopin study.'

Big and broad, Adam stepped forward and with a gesture he silenced everyone. Strong and commanding, he drew Julie to his side, and as though she drew strength from the warm hand which covered her own, Julie straightened up and smiled politely.

A fair, fragile-looking girl, with softly swaying brown hair, Julie made her way to the piano. There was music in her every movement, but Julie did not realise this. Nor did she see the almost sad, softening of Adam Rich's eyes as she began to bring out the haunting rippling melody of the

Impromptu. It was a piece warm with colour and fluency and containing a certain wistful sorrow and emotion which seemed to suit Julie's artistic temperament. Sweet and yet just a little uncertain, the notes seemed to fall from Julie's fingers as though created in her own soul.

Everyone in the room was now held in rapt attention. Critical eyes grew more astonished and astonishment gave way to appraisal. Here was talent indeed! Eyebrow after eyebrow rose, lips parted, throats worked with emotion as Julie, alone and confident now in her own world of music, held them enthralled. All that existed for Julie now was the enchantment of her own art. Everything, everyone forgotten, she lived only for her music. She wished only for the innocent, yet ecstatic copulation of her fingertips with the keyboard. She played not only with expertise but with her heart.

Listening, Adam Rich felt a thrill no sharp-edged scalpel had ever offered him, a challenge, which made him straighten up and brace his shoulders as his gaze was once again drawn to the slight girl who held everyone transfixed, a girl whose very soul seemed to fill the room. A soul more provocative to him than any physical challenge.

As though she read his mind, Susie Tulip moved a little closer so that her thigh brushed Adam's and, laying her head against his shoulder, she murmured, 'I suppose it's great if you like the stuff.'

Straightening up again, Adam Rich said something under his breath, something which made Susie give him a long, hard look, and then turn to Julie, who was just bringing the Impromptu to a close.

For a few seconds the small audience seemed to remain in a state of trance, then they rose to their feet to applaud the girl whose eyes had turned to Adam. The babble of conversation rose. Julie decided against playing again. And then Adam was at her side.

'That was wonderful,' he told her. 'Thank

you, Julie. Perhaps you would play again later, but now you must come and have dinner with us. My sister...'

'Darling!'

It was Susie and again she clung possessively to Adam's arm.

'Darling,' she began again, her eyes a little bleary. 'Elisha is waiting, so do give Nurse Singer her cheque. I'm sure she must be relieved to have got that over. We're not all quite so technical. For parties I must say I prefer the bad, blaring pop—'

Cheque? Then she had been engaged! Hired by the surgeon to play for his guests. Used as an instrument, no doubt, to gain him prestige. The distress in Julie's eyes reflected painfully in Adam's as she turned to stare at him.

'Be kind, darling,' Susie purred. 'Give her a little extra. She's brave as well as clever.' A silly smile, a hiccup and then, 'She's either brave or deluded. She must know by now that we are not exactly gluttons for culture.'

A firm hand launched Susie off into a

mass of throbbing bodies; affected, trendy, beautiful, and all working hard at enjoying themselves.

'She's had too much to drink, damn her,' Adam said in a dangerous tone. 'I can only apologise.'

'Don't bother,' Julie said in a tight voice. 'I really must go. You don't need to throw in a dinner, Adam. Just send me that cheque.'

'Julie!'

The genuine distress in his tone, the anger in his eyes momentarily detained Julie. She stared back at him again.

'You are not going,' he said harshly. 'I won't let you. I want you to meet one or two of my special friends. They want to meet you.'

'That's too bad,' Julie flung back. 'I charge for interviews.'

'You're being ridiculous! Childish! Also, do you wish to make me look ridiculous.'

Julie laughed back at him. 'Then you would at least know how it feels,' she shouted above the blare of pop music.

'Oh, so you're going?' Susie appeared again, looking all ruffled and breathless, and yet still very stunning in a green chiffon dress which at least covered her knees if nothing else. 'Well, perhaps next time you will have,' hiccup, 'the good sense to bring a bottle instead of your harp...'

Staring at her, Julie felt a repugnant emotion well up inside her. She hated them all, all Adam Rich's beautiful friends. She hated them because she was not one of them, she hated their cheap sophistication, their lack of natural charm.

And most of all she hated Adam Rich.

'I'll drive you back, Julie.'

It was Adam who spoke, but Julie would not look at him.

Thrusting his hand from her arm, she quickly made her way to the door and then through a blur of angry tears out into the dark night.

★ ★ ★ ★

'And you mean to say you had to get a bus home?' Lynn exploded wrathfully. 'God in heaven!'

Sitting on her bed, rocking with fury, Julie watched her friend pace the floor like a caged cat.

'That's crazy!' Lynn went on wildly. 'You did the wrong thing, Julie. Everyone knows that Susie has a liking for the liquor. She must have been drunk. But even when she's drunk, she's clever. Did you expect her to stand back and watch you captivate her surgeon with a rattle over the keys. Oh, for heaven's sake, Julie, I wish you were a bit more worldly. In any case, I don't believe the Prof hired you. That's crazy.'

'Forget it,' Julie said in a steely voice. 'I intend to. Besides, I always hated parties. I'm a bit of a loner, I guess. And you were right, Lynn. I should have had more sense than to get involved with the Prof.'

Flopping down beside her friend, Lynn encouraged, 'Come on, you're not going to bed with your clothes on. What about a cuppa. I've got some tea-bags. Well, two drying behind the door.'

'No, thanks,' Julie answered, trying to smile. 'But you can make me laugh. Any news from the battlefront?'

Lynn giggled. 'Yes,' she laughed, 'remember that dude of a junior on Men's Surgical?'

Julie nodded, absently.

'She was left on the ward at lunchtime and the surgeon happened to do a round. Guess what she said they had in bed three? A transplant of hernia!'

At last Julie broke out into peels of laughter. 'Can you believe it?' Lynn rocked against the wall. 'Apparently the whole procession keeled over... Transplant of hernia!'

'Poor kid!' Julie sympathised and her eyes turned grave again.

'And here is something else that might cheer you up,' Lynn put in quickly and, standing up, she took a letter from her pocket and tossed it on to the bed. 'A letter for you,' she said, grinning. 'From the London College of Music.'

'What!' Julie caught her breath. 'How do you know?'

'It's stamped on the envelope.'

Julie tore it open.

'Well, what does it say?' Lynn enquired after a few moments.

Julie could not answer at once, she could only stare at her friend.

'Bad news?' Lynn pulled a face.

This time Julie shook her head, and suddenly her face came to life; colour flooded up from her throat, her blue eyes sparkled and grew moist. 'I can't believe it,' she breathed. 'Oh, Lynn, I just can't believe it.'

'What can't you believe?' Lynn's voice grew impatient.

'It's from one of my old tutors,' Julie gasped incredulously. 'He's actually got me an engagement with an orchestra which is to play here in Newcastle. They're doing the Fourth Concerto! It's my favourite! And this is a chance in a million! Lynn, it's wonderful news.'

'Will you get paid?'

'Yes.'

'In peanuts, I suppose.'

'What does it matter? Oh, Lynn, I'm suddenly so happy.'

'Well, I'm glad to hear it. But what about the big money? Have you heard any more?'

Julie shook her head. 'I can't think of it,' she laughed shakily. 'I can't think of anything but this coming concert. I can't even think of Adam.'

'So you're cured. Well, that was quick. Thank God for the London College. I thought you were going into a decline five minutes ago.' Lynn moved towards the door. 'Don't forget,' she called, 'I want a seat at that concert. And when you're famous I'm your friend. Don't forget that either.'

'I won't!' At last Julie stood up. 'To hell with the Prof. And to hell with his bilateral salpingo-oöphorectomies ... I'm going to play with an orchestra!'

'Well, bully for you,' Lynn laughed happily, and she opened the door. 'And I'm going to bed.'

'I hear you were out with David Whittaker last night,' Julie teased, her eyes suddenly full of affection for her long-suffering friend.

'That's right,' Lynn called back round the door. 'And if that's sex, you can stuff it.'

After the door closed after Lynn, Julie undressed and pulled on her cotton nightie, got into bed and read her letter again. She had to let the agent know at once ... she must state her fee. And they were playing her beloved Fourth.

Eventually Julie's eyes closed and very soon she was being led on to the concert stage. In her dreams she bowed to the thunderous applause of her audience. There was no humiliation now, no wounded pride ... only a necessary and professional show of humility.

FOUR

During the following week Julie managed to concentrate on her work, seeking refuge in the Sluice Room whenever a procession headed by the Prof came into sight. All her off-duty time was given to practising for the forthcoming concert. And, struggling determinedly, Julie was somehow able to keep Adam from her mind. Anger, regret, she knew never fortified anyone and at this particular time she needed all her confidence. She had, she told herself, to walk on to that concert stage with all the professional panache she could muster. She had to keep up her spirits. No man was going to make her sink ten feet deep in gloom. And so Julie deliberately ended her practice sessions with another concerto dear to her heart, the Saint-Saëns G minor. This stimulated her to greater effort. It never failed to revive her drive. Also, unknown to Julie, it never failed to stop any nurses passing by, to stand and listen, breath held, to notes which held both romantic sadness and carnival spriteliness.

A talk over the telephone to her tutor at the London College of Music also did much to restore Julie's pride and fill her with excitement. 'I know you will be a success,' he had assured her. 'I know also that we will see you back here one of these days. Meanwhile, my dear, do not miss an opportunity.'

And now she was to have a chance to prove herself. She was to play with a real orchestra. To a real audience. Not a mob of morons! As Julie hurried back to the ward her thoughts now returned to the letter she had received from her mother. The solicitors had written to her, urging her to press her daughter to reply to their communication without delay.

And so a decision was to be made. Lynn's

forged report might yet have to be sent, Julie thought anxiously, as she hurried along the corridor to Eleven.

Something was wrong! There was Sister Grey, like affliction at the gate!

'Nurse Baron must be sick,' Sister Grey shrilled the moment Julie started down the annex corridor. 'I'll ring Matron. Meanwhile, Nurse Singer, you had better go to theatre.'

To theatre! Julie's face turned bright red. Helplessly, she stared back at Sister Grey. She had never worked in an operating theatre. She would not know what to do. Suddenly she went cold with fear.

'You'll be all right,' Sister Grey said briskly. 'Don't look so terrified, Singer. Sister Pratt will keep an eye on you. It's just a matter of counting and checking swabs. Making yourself generally useful.' Widening her eyes, she added jokingly, 'I don't suppose they'll ask you to operate.'

Sister's humour, thought Julie, was about as funny as a broken jaw. She found it impossible to raise even a dutiful smile.

'You'll keep off the Prof's toes, won't you?' Whittaker teased as he bounded up to them, already clad in theatre boots and rubber apron, the theatre board in his hand.

Julie ignored him and so Whittaker turned to Sister Grey with apologetic eyes. With a shrug he told her, 'The Prof wants the D and Cs after the first salpingectomy, Sister. Sorry.'

Sister Grey mumbled something under her breath and then raised her eyes to the theatre trolley which was rumbling down the annex with Freddy the porter whistling behind it.

'Off you go then, Singer,' she said and with a flick of her hand she moved Julie on.

The lift whirred down to the first corridor and with it Julie, who stood shivering. She was to watch an operation! Work at close quarters with the Prof! Adam ... who had such a devastating effect upon her. She broke out into a sweat. Her legs felt like spaghetti.

Another shock was in store for Julie, for the moment she pushed open the theatre doors she came face to face with the Prof, who was crossing from the Sterilising Room to the Anaesthetist's.

'Nurse Singer? Julie?'

She saw him start, a dull flush spread up below his dark skin. But it was with a cool, controlled voice that he said, 'Well, Nurse, what can we do for you?'

'I've been sent to theatre, sir,' Julie answered formally. 'Nurse Baron has gone off sick. I'm to take her place.'

He stood watching her for a moment, revealing nothing of the thoughts behind his dark, brilliant eyes. 'Well,' he went on again at last and his eyes were cynical now as they held Julie's, 'come and enjoy the show. Although I warn you now, Nurse, once my theatre doors close, there'll be no running away.'

'Nurse Singer!'

Julie spun round. Sister Pratt had appeared in the doorway of the Sterilising

Room. At once, Julie explained, 'Sister sent me. I've never been in theatre before.'

'Hurry up, then, Nurse,' Sister Pratt said smartly. 'You'll soon learn. But not standing there gaping. Get changed and scrubbed up. Nurse Roberts will show you what you have to do.'

For a brief moment Julie's eyes met Adam's and, to her chagrin, she saw that he was smiling.

Nurse Roberts, a tall, efficient-looking nurse, led Julie away and very soon she was shrouded in theatre gown, mask and cap and feeling about as useless as a mummy.

'Don't worry,' Roberts said. 'You'll soon get the hang of it.'

Julie gave the nurse a quick grateful smile, then she heard the theatre doors slam shut and her heart gave another great lurch. She was frightened.

Yet twenty minutes later Julie was checking and re-checking the swabs as directed, calling out the number and eyeing the nurse who wrote it up on the board. An operation was in progress. Now Julie's eyes strayed as far as the instrument trolley and Sister Pratt who stood by it, sharp-eyed and efficient, a gleaming instrument raised in readiness. Another intake of breath and Julie glanced at the anaesthetist. Finally she raised her eyes to the students who stood back from the operating table. So far she had not been able to make herself look down at the patient but she could hear her deep, controlled breathing. Her eyes still focused, Julie wondered if Adam could hear the terrified beat of her heart.

It seemed that he did for now he was saying in a deliberate tone, 'It could have been worse, Nurse. You could have been my patient.' All eyes were on Julie, for they knew the Prof's dry humour. Everyone was smiling, everyone but Julie, who stood as straight as a stick and poker-faced.

Julie heard the click of metal against metal, she caught the flash of a bloodied scalpel, and then Adam's voice was droning, 'Are you going to faint, Nurse Singer?' And once again the onlookers smiled.

Julie could not answer him. Everything was spinning–'

'Find yourself a suitable place, Nurse,' the deep voice went on. 'Find it before you do faint. Away from my feet, please.'

Again the students tittered. Julie kept her eyes on a lotion bowl. She would not faint! She would not give him that satisfaction. She bit her lip beneath the mask, she rubbed one ankle harshly against the other. She was not going to be stepped over like a bundle of rags.

Pain revived her; Julie kept her feet. And her interest grew. Adam began to lecture to the students quietly as he worked. She glanced at him now and, forgetting his sarcasm she felt a rush of pride. He was brilliant! He *was* a miracle man! At last Julie's gaze lowered to the patient. And suddenly fear gave way to astonishment; her throat worked with emotion. Adam was also a great conductor! With his hands, he restored to perfect harmony a body fallen in discord. He was wonderful! He was magnificent!

And he was staring at her. Shouting, 'Swab, Nurse! We don't want the patient to bleed to death.'

Another swab marked up and Julie breathed again. They were nearly finished now; Whittaker the houseman was helping to sew up. Julie was conscious of Adam giving her another hard stare but this time she kept her eyes hard on the incision.

'Well done, Nurse,' she heard him say. 'Perhaps you're not the sensitive creature you would have us believe?'

This time Julie's head jerked back angrily. Her eyes met Adam's fiercely but again she bit her lip.

'So,' the Prof began again, but just then a loud crash from the back of the theatre drew their attention. 'So,' he continued stingingly now, 'I see we have the joker with us.' With an abrupt angry gesture, he suddenly stripped off his rubber gloves and threw them across the floor. 'Sister,' he called in a harsh, raised voice, 'will you please get that clown a fresh jacket. A strait one preferably. Also I refuse to have him in this theatre again.' Beginning to wash up at the sinks, he eyed Julie through the wall mirror, then roughly he called, 'I'll have my coffee now, Sister. Before the D and Cs start rolling in. And this morning I'll have it black. Strong.'

In the Sterilising Room Julie tried to make herself useful but everyone was so busy that she felt she was merely getting in their way.

'Fill the steriliser,' an alert, dark-skinned nurse called to her. 'With lotion bowls, darling. The big steriliser. On your right.'

Thankful for something to do, Julie set about filling the steriliser. Then Sister Pratt barged in, her expression pleased. 'That's right, Nurse,' she called to Julie. 'You'll soon get the hang of it. The nurses will tell you what to do. But please don't stand quite so close to the Prof. Give him plenty of elbow room.'

'Yes, Sister.' Julie gave Sister Pratt a quick, grateful smile. The nurses began to chat with her, and when everything was under way for the next op they began to relax a little.

'Four D and Cs and then a hysterectomy,' the dark-skinned girl said again. 'That's not too bad. We should be finished by one.'

Julie stood back to let her pass and then gasped with shock and spun round because she had knocked something over.

'Gawd!' cried one of the nurses. 'Get Sister's blouse out of the way!'

It was too late; a bottle of powerful acid which Julie had inadvertently spilt now ran over the bench and dripped on to the collar of the blouse which had been lying over the back of a wooden chair.

'Oh, Gawd,' cried the nurse again and she stood back to stare at Julie in terror. 'It's Sister's favourite blouse,' she groaned. 'She was going to give it a rinse through. Oh, Singer, you're certainly for it. That blouse cost the earth. It's pure silk!'

Julie stood transfixed, as though cornered by a cobra. She could not speak.

'What is it?' Sister Pratt breezed in again. Then her eyes went to the chair and she stopped dead in her tracks. Her eyes glistening now, she looked like a stoat in a hen-house. 'What's this?' she burst out. 'Who did this?' she shrilled. Furiously now, she snatched up her blouse, examined it and then tossed it down with dismay.

Only the rumbling of the steriliser was to be heard now, only glances of dismay were exchanged as the nurses edged back before Sister Pratt's wrath.

Julie stood forward, her face as white as the tiled wall behind her. 'I'm sorry, Sister,' she began tremulously, 'I...'

'You did this? You've been in my theatre an hour and you've done this?' Sister Pratt's eyes blazed mercilessly into Julie's.

'I'm sorry, Sister.' For a moment Julie's greatest urge was to take to her heels. Luckily, the door opened again and the Prof peered into the room.

'Nice coffee, Sister,' he called amicably and just for a brief moment his eyes sought

Julie's. Instantly he straightened up. 'Something wrong, Sister?' he enquired, and his dark eyes narrowed curiously.

Sister Pratt's lips remained sealed, but her gaze went first to her blouse, then accusingly to Julie.

'I spilt some acid on Sister's blouse,' Julie explained desperately. 'I've ruined it. I've said I'm sorry...' Tears began to blur her vision, her throat was filling up. Unable to say more, she turned away.

Painfully the other nurses looked on.

'I see,' the Prof murmured, frowning at the sight of Julie's distress.

Numb with shock, Julie did not hear Adam's exclamation, nor did she see his expression as he crossed the room to her. But she did feel a strong, comforting arm come down on her shoulders and now she turned and stared up at him in astonishment. Her lips quivered, and had there not been three equally astounded nurses looking in she knew she would have fallen into his arms and broken down.

'An unfortunate accident, no doubt,' the Prof said in a dominant, masculine voice. 'But not one to stop the show. Carry on, Sister. And, rest assured, I will consider it a privilege if you will allow me to replace the ruined blouse with one equally beautiful.' Only Sister Pratt saw the Prof's smile as he turned from Julie to address her, and she found it completely disarming. 'I know exactly what would suit you, Sister,' he teased charmingly. 'You can safely leave this shopping expedition to me. You'll see, I can do more than use a scalpel. In fact,' he laughed low in his throat, 'at one time I rather fancied having a boutique in Bond Street. But those,' he added with a grin, 'were the days when my aspirations were high.'

'The hysterectomy has arrived, sir,' Sister Pratt said stonily and averting her eyes, for she had long fancied the surgeon. 'Do you want her on the table?'

'I guess so.' Adam stroked his chin and then momentarily glanced back at Julie.

Then with a smile touching his lips he marched back into the Anaesthetist's Room.

So she was not going to be thrown to the sharks! Julie began to breathe again. Glancing at the dark-skinned nurse, she asked shakily, 'What do I do now?'

'It seems you can do nothing wrong,' the nurse returned ironically and under her breath. 'Had that been one of us we'd have been out on our backsides.'

'Nurse!' Sister Pratt popped her head round the door again and eyed Julie. 'Come and help to get the patient on the table,' she called. 'Then you can scrub up again.'

'Yes, Sister.' Julie hurried to do her bidding, but she knew that had it not been for Adam's charm she would have been on her way to Matron's office.

Theatre finished at one o'clock and at three o'clock Julie was back on the ward, checking the blood pressure and drip flow of one of the patients who had undergone major surgery. As usual after ops the ward was oddly quiet; no visitors, no jolly students and Simpson respectfully but aggravatingly doing rounds on her toes. Eleven was like a cathedral close.

Bella had been drawing a duster over the medicine chest in the centre of the ward but now she paused to grin at Simpson, who had stopped to have a word with Julie.

'How did you get on in theatre, Nurse?' Simpson enquired in a suitably sympathetic voice. 'I expect you were scared?'

Julie kept her eye on the blood pressure gauge. 'Not at all,' she answered levelly. 'It was a super experience, Simpson. I feel as though I really know what is going on now.'

'By jingles, but you don't,' Bella put in cheekily. 'You want to keep your eye on the auxiliary, Nurse. She's a regular ward-comber. Goes home every night with that great bag of hers packed.'

'Either keep your voice down or shut up,' Simpson retaliated, her round, middle-aged face suddenly blown out and as red as a pomegranate. 'Have you no sense, Bella? No respect for the patients?'

'What's wrong with them?' Bella tossed back loftily and with an air of experience. 'They're not here for sympathy. They're here to be cured. And they are.'

Julie sighed as she watched Simpson follow Bella down the ward to the kitchen, and a few moments later she heard their voices raised in battle. Then the ward doors swung open again and David Whittaker, wearing a white jacket over his T-shirt and denim trousers, came swiftly towards her.

'How is she?' he asked at once, his eyes hard on the patient's moist, ashen face. 'She's lost quite a bit of blood.' After checking the drip himself he turned to Julie. 'Blood pressure?'

'Rising...'

'Good. Stay with her.'

'Of course!'

'Everyone else all right?'

'So far...'

'And you?' Whittaker grinned at Julie.

'I'm fine.' Julie frowned up at him. 'Why do you ask?' she said. 'Do I look ill?'

'No, but you had a lucky escape. That was a real smart move on the old man's part, Nurse Singer. He really has a soft spot for you. Don't imagine Pratt was fooled. She'll keep her eye on you. She's fancied the Prof for years.'

'Is there any need to call him an old man,' Julie defended fiercely. 'He's certainly a brilliant man.'

'Oh!' Whittaker grinned. 'So I touched a nerve. You fancy him. Perhaps you'd like to talk about it ... preferably over a drink in the Black Bull. I'm a good listener.'

'I don't need a confidant,' Julie told him loftily. 'I can look after myself, thank you, Doctor.'

'Maybe, but I'm always ready to play Sir Galahad should the need arise.' His eyes ranged over Julie as he added, 'You're a lovely bird, Julie. But not a worldly wise one. And so I make this point of warning you. You're not in his class, pet. Or hers! And you know who I mean. They could eat you ... on toast.'

'Oh, shut up! See to your patients.'

David Whittaker had already wandered on to the next bed. 'And now, Mrs Fox,' he began gently, and as he took the woman's hand, 'how are you? Just coming round, eh?'

The woman smiled sleepily, raised her eyes and lowered them again.

'You're going to be fine.' Again Whittaker patted the limp hand.

He's nice, Julie thought as she watched him. And he is right. When it comes to landing men I'm certainly not in Susie's class. In fact, where men are concerned I've had no experience at all. How could I? I've spent most of my time rattling off scales, thundering out arpeggios. I've never had any kind of relationship with a man. Or a woman for that matter. Lynn is my first real friend.

'Nurse Singer!'

Julie set down her patient's pulse chart, exchanged a quick smile with Whittaker and then set off down the ward.

'Yes, Sister?'

'You go to first tea, Nurse Singer. And when you get back start the temps. Dixon can do the round.'

'Yes, Sister.'

'Off you go, then.'

Before Julie could move Sister Grey detained her again, with a smile and congratulatory, 'I hear you kept your head in theatre this morning, Nurse. Well done.'

'Thank you, Sister.' A flush of pleasure spread over Julie's fine features. Pleased, she hurriedly made her way out of the ward and out into the main hospital corridor. It was praise indeed when it came from Sister Grey. On a theatre day! She suddenly felt elated; she wanted to sing, to skip... Again Julie felt a rush of pride.

Then she saw them. Adam and Susie Tulip were standing in the corridor ahead of her, talking together in low voices, Adam's arm about Susie's shoulder. She heard Susie laugh softly, provocatively, then she saw her look up into Adam's eyes. And now Adam was looking down into Susie's and he was laughing softly, in a low, intimate way.

Her legs suddenly like lead, Julie walked on, praying with all her might that they would not notice her. Now elation gave way to the misery of jealousy. Suddenly she felt as though she had been sentenced to a long, silent martyrdom. Suddenly she knew, Adam Rich was not for her. Averting her eyes, straight-backed, she walked on.

'Nurse Singer!'

Grave-eyed, Julie turned to acknowledge them.

'See you...' Susie Tulip murmured, as her eyes drew away from Adam's, as her fingers trailed away from his. Then just for a second she straightened up and her eyes met Julie's with a mocking, almost amused expression.

'So you didn't clutter up my floor this morning, Julie,' Adam Rich said, and he smiled down into Julie's pained eyes.

'No, sir.'

'Then you must pay us another visit.'

'Nurse Baron should be back by next Theatre Day, sir.'

'What a pity. I thought you and I might have inadvertently got together again.' Changing his tone to one which held both anger and resentment, he went on, 'I'd still like a chance to explain what happened that other night. I'm not used to guests barging out of my home.'

'There is nothing to explain, sir.'

'For God's sake! Don't call me sir.'

The impatience in his voice made Julie wince. Her face stiff with fury, she raised her eyes to his, then suddenly she made a movement to go.

'No. You won't escape so easily this time.' Adam Rich caught Julie's wrist with a hard, determined hand and drew her back.

'Don't be silly, Julie,' he said. 'Damn it all – I won't let you.'

'What is there to explain?' she asked, and she lowered her eyes again.

'You must have realised that I could not embarrass my guests, Julie,' he said in a firm voice. 'And what could I do when you so rudely barged out?'

She could not answer. She had barged out rudely.

'Now I can at least apologise,' he went on, a look of gentleness coming again into his eyes as he scanned Julie's youthful face. 'I should have realised that you would require a fee. A professional fee.'

Their eyes met again, Julie's puzzled, his uncertain.

'I imagined you were my guest,' he went on before she could say anything. 'And that you would not take it amiss if I asked you to play for my friends. It was Susie who sensibly brought this lamentable mistake to my notice. I must confess, I would not expect any one of my associates to work without a fee. I should never have expected you to play without one. So, if you must give the death sentence to a friendship which had distinct possibilities, then what can I do?'

Susie! Clever Susie! David Whittaker was right. She was not in Susie's class when it came to using her head. She looked up at

Adam again, then her gaze went down to his hands. 'Please, Adam,' she said in a small voice. 'I would hate it so much if you sent me that cheque.'

'And I would hate it so much if I thought you were never going to play for me again, Julie.'

They stared at each other for a moment, then he smiled and gently lifted her chin, and Julie was sure he would have kissed her had it not been for a noisy mob of nurses suddenly appearing on the corridor.

★ ★ ★ ★

The day of the concert arrived and in the morning Julie went to the rehearsal at the concert hall, which was in the centre of the city. The conductor, a middle-aged man with dreamy eyes and an old world courtesy, greeted Julie with kindness and a certain amount of puzzlement. 'We wanted someone young,' he explained. 'And you were very highly commended.' After the rehearsal he ceremoniously kissed Julie's hand and told her, 'That was splendid. You are a superb pianist, my dear. It shames me to know that you are working in a hospital.'

That night Lynn helped Julie to dress and, when Julie was ready, her hair freshly washed and set, her make-up carefully applied, she slipped on her tiered chiffon dress. It was blue, the exact shade of Julie's eyes, and Lynn sank back against the wall of the bedroom to sigh with admiration. 'You look gorgeous!' she breathed. 'Honestly, Julie ... it won't matter how you play.' Over a lump in her throat Lynn added, 'And good luck. You deserve it.'

'Why don't you come with me,' Julie complained, as she glanced in her mirror again. 'I wouldn't mind you being there, Lynn. I couldn't stand one other familiar face, but, truly, I'd like you to come.'

'Not on your life, darling,' Lynn breathed. 'I'm not a glutton for punishment. I'll wait in the chippy on the other side of the road. I'll be there if anything goes wrong ... but it won't. I'm sure of that.' With another long sigh, 'You'll probably be famous overnight, Julie. I may never see you again.'

'You're crazy,' Julie laughed back. 'Come on. At least you can see me into the taxi. It's due at any moment.'

'Just a minute,' Lynn called, and she suddenly looked rather guilty.

'What is it?' Julie glanced back.

'You don't need to worry any more about hearing from your solicitors.'

'What do you mean?' Julie's throat worked.

'I sent that report to them. By this time it will be filed away. You're in the clear, Julie. So when do we order our first Rolls?'

'Lynn!' Julie groaned, and suddenly she did not know whether to laugh or cry. 'What a time to tell me.'

'A good time, I guessed,' Lynn grinned. 'Now that we're halfway to a fortune, you can relax – and I'll read a bit more about that nurse who went on holiday to this place where she swam in a fabulous pool and trampled on some fabulous millionaire's toe...' Julie was not listening. She did not know whether she was pleased or sorry, scared or relieved. But it was in a slightly irritable tone that she said, 'Wait for me, Lynn. I'm coming now.' As they walked along Virgins' Alley together she said anxiously, 'I just hope we've done the right thing, Lynn. We could end up in trouble. You shouldn't have done it.'

'By the time they find out,' Lynn encouraged blithely, 'we'll be on our dream island. Stop worrying, Julie. You couldn't make the decision so I did it for you, that's all.'

* * * *

The moment Julie met the other performers she forgot everything but her music. Excited, thrilled to be with her own kind of people – people who understood music – Julie, when at last the small hall was packed and the lights were dimmed, walked on to the stage with the aplomb of a true artist.

The audience applauded wildly, touched by something else they recognised ... the pianist's good will, her youthful wish to please, her obvious intelligence and natural beauty. And the fact that Julie had done her best to look attractive, all made for their evening's entertainment.

A tall, handsome man wearing a velvet jacket took a deep breath and leaned forward a little as though to observe Julie more fully, while at his side a beautiful woman sat tense, wary.

Julie did not see them, her eyes were on the conductor's baton. And then with split-second timing she came in with the theme. And again she felt the jubilation of doing what she was meant to do – play with an orchestra. And within moments the audience had sat back, content, silent, en-thralled.

It was a piece that opened quietly and without the expected bombast of a piano concerto, Julie playing the first five bars of the theme. And at once every eye was upon the slim, beautiful girl at the piano.

Julie gave herself up to Beethoven's Fourth Piano Concerto, and alone in her world of music, she now brought about a miracle of loveliness. With skilled and sensitive fingers she wove a pattern of sounds. Sounds warm, colourful and with the fluency of sheer poetry. It was a lyrical piece, yet with a rich background of emotion: sorrow, anger and compassion. And as Julie played she seemed herself to become part of the beauty of her music.

In her heart, Julie knew she was playing for Adam. It had been written from the soul of a man whom love had made both the happiest and unhappiest of men, and now her own interpretation of feeling held every face in the hall rapt, every eye still or lowered.

With the second movement, the *Andante con moto,* the emotional intensity grew and, as though momentarily seeking relief, Julie glanced in the direction of her audience.

And saw Adam! It was a shock, and she lost her timing. A gasp from the audience ... and her fingers stumbled. Yet with the skill and sympathy of the conductor Julie managed to continue and again the audience sank back spellbound.

Her heart full, Julie played on. For a brief time she knew she had Adam in her power. With her music she had captivated him. She would never forget that expression on his face. With her music, if nothing else, she would haunt him.

And then came the end and Julie stood up to receive the homage of her conductor and the applause of the audience and just for a moment her eyes again sought Adam's.

And her heart leapt up again, for it was not surprise she saw in Adam's dark, intelligent eyes now but adoration. Alas, she thought, as she bowed once again, the surgeon's love was not for herself but for her art. He so obviously felt a kind of adoration for the lovely woman who stood next to him. For Susie Tulip, who once again clung to his arm possessively.

A bouquet now and then Julie left the stage followed by the conductor. As usual, a party was being held for the members of the orchestra and, as Julie stood chatting to the conductor and his very pleasant wife and the violinist and his girlfriend, her gaze began to wander. And again Julie's heart stood still. Again she looked into Adam's eyes ... for he was standing at the opposite side of the room, regarding her steadily, a drink in one hand and a cigar in the other.

Julie's throat worked sensitively, she drew her eyes away from his but even then she knew he was halfway across the room to her.

'Julie!'

She turned to him and he raised his glass.

'Congratulations,' he said in a deep, masculine voice, one which never failed to make Julie's heart turn over. And with a disarming smile he said, 'After such a performance I take my hat off to you. That was superb.'

'Thank you, Adam.'

His Christian name slipped from her tongue before she could stop it and now she saw an expression of pleasure leap into his eyes. 'I could hardly call you sir or Prof on such an occasion,' she retracted dizzily.

'And I could hardly call you Nurse after hearing you play so magnificently.' A pause while his eyes rested on Julie were gentle. 'For once,' he began again, 'I hardly know what to say. Only, Julie, that you continue to amaze me.' Smiling again, he raised his glass and exclaimed, 'All those notes! All that variation...'

'And I couldn't remember the percentage for a douche lotion,' Julie put in, and for a moment her eyes were accusing.

His eyes grew quizzical. 'What are you doing at St George's?' he asked in a deep breath. 'Julie, you were never meant for Ward Eleven.'

'Yes, just what are you doing at St George's?' a sharp voice broke in and Susie Tulip, looking more glamorous than ever in a brown velvet suit and cream silk blouse, appeared from behind a group of guests. 'I've been asking myself that all night. If I could play like you, Nurse, I wouldn't spend my time listening to wheezy chests.'

'Like the other girls,' Julie replied carefully. 'I'm training to be a good nurse. I've always admired them,' she went on as her feeling of guilt grew. 'They give so much.'

'I'd say you were wasting your time,' Susie put in directly, and as she slipped her arm through Adam's. 'But, no doubt, someone will discover you and you'll be whisked away...' But it will not be Adam who whisks you away, Susie's bright eyes inferred as she turned to smile at Julie. Then, giving Adam another bright smile, she urged, 'Darling, you must come and meet this friend of mine. She plays with the orchestra. I can't believe it. I haven't seen her since schooldays.'

'You go ahead,' Adam said assertively, his eyes on Julie again. 'There is something I must say to Julie...'

'Can't it wait?'

Julie saw Susie's eyes flash dangerously and, not wishing to cause Adam more embarrassment, she said swiftly, 'I'm afraid it must wait, Adam. I really must mingle. Look, there is the conductor beckoning to me again... Sorry.'

★ ★ ★ ★

An hour later Julie climbed into her taxi and sat back to savour the feeling of success. She had played well, been congratulated over and over again. More than ever now she was determined to get her SRN and return to the London College of Music. She got on with the nurses but they made her feel inadequate; she was ill at ease working in a large training school. Also it took everything out of her; every night it seemed she went to bed exhausted with the sheer effort of what the other nurses took to be a simple day's work. Lynn had told her she was too conscientious, that she got too involved. And, as usual, she guessed that Lynn was right.

But tonight she had been involved only with her music. Not for a long time had she been so happy. She wasn't tired at all! One day she would be a celebrated concert pianist, she told herself on a fresh wave of elation.

It was dark when the taxi wound its way up the drive to Out-Patients' Hall. Julie paid the driver and then quickly made her way towards the brilliantly lit entrance. She was halfway across the courtyard when a heavy hand came down on her arm and she gasped with shock.

'Julie!'

It was Adam again! In astonishment she stared back at him. 'What a shock you gave me,' she gasped.

'I'm sorry, but I'm determined to talk to you.' Taking her hand firmly, he said, 'Come over to my car, Julie. This can't wait. I've made a decision.'

'Have you been waiting for me?' Julie queried tremulously as Adam bundled her into his car and closed the door before getting in himself. 'How did you know how long I would be?'

'I didn't,' he said, sitting back to stare at her. 'I've been waiting here for over an hour.'

'But why?'

'Because your playing tonight was a revelation, Julie,' he said with growing emotion. 'And I consider it my duty to do something about this talent you have. I can't watch you splash about with douche cans when I know your potential as a musician. It would be morally wrong. Criminal!'

Julie looked at him, unable to think of anything to say. He looked so handsome, so distinguished, so interested. Suddenly she wanted to throw her arms about him, tell him the truth. Instead, she tried to force a little humour into her voice as she accused, 'You're really determined to get rid of me, aren't you, Adam?'

'No, I'm not.' He sat back now against the car door, staring at Julie in the same manner as he might consider a new and challenging case. Then he sighed and, taking Julie's hand, he stared down at it and told her with emotion and with a growing passion, 'You were never meant for the world of blood and sepsis, Julie. The surgeon may give a man the use of his limbs but you, Julie ... you can give a heart wings. You have the power to make an ordinary humdrum body shudder with ecstasy. With the touch of your fingertips you can awaken a million nerve endings... What more can I say?'

'I'd like you to be a bit more complimentary about my nursing capabilities,' Julie retaliated tremulously. 'Because I am determined to become an SRN. What could be more noble?' she added because she thought it might give strength to her case. 'And, Adam,' she added suddenly, overcome by shyness, 'I must say I thought you were wonderful in theatre. I never realised – you made it all feel worthwhile. The hard work – the–'

He smiled again, slowly, withdrawing his hand from hers. 'I can see I'm going to have to be brutal,' he laughed gently. 'I admire your dedication, Julie, but I have a suggestion to make. If it's money that's bothering you, I'd be quite willing to help. I realise that you'd need to study in London, at perhaps the College of Music. I have a contact there. I would also consider it a privilege if you would let me give you some aid financially.'

'Money!' It was Julie's turn to draw back from him. 'I don't want your money,' she told him with a rush of indignation. 'I've told you I'm determined to be an SRN.'

'Julie,' he began again, and this time he took both her hands in his and, as his eyes probed hers, he said levelly, 'I have a feeling that something is troubling you? Are you telling me the truth?'

'Of course I'm telling you the truth,' she told him bravely. 'I want to get my SRN.' And closing her eyes because she could not bear his expression, she laughed, 'If I wanted a sugar daddy, I wouldn't choose you. I have certainly no intention of making up a trio with Dr Tulip.'

Startled by Julie's words, he sat back, a puzzled look in his eyes. 'That's it, then,' he said after a painful silence. 'It seems I'm wasting my time.'

Still Julie could not raise her eyes to his but she heard the car door open and then felt the hard grip on her arm as he helped her out and then escorted her across the courtyard to the Out-Patients' Hall.

'Goodnight,' he said stiffly, and that was all.

'What's wrong, then?' Lynn enquired ten minutes later. 'Did it crash? Didn't they like your sinatras?'

'Sonata!' Julie flung. 'For goodness' sake, Lynn! Besides, it was a concerto. And it didn't crash. I was great! You should have heard the applause.'

'Well, that's marvellous. Shall I open our last bottle of hooch?'

Julie shook her head and then drew off her dress. 'Professor Rich was there,' she said in a small voice.

'Oh, I see ... So you're thinking about him again and not the sinatra ... sorry, concerto.'

Turning to her friend, Julie now told her the full story. 'And he was waiting for me at Out-Patients,' she finally breathed. 'He'd been waiting for ages, Lynn. He offered to help me. To aid me financially so that I can go back to college.'

'Did he really,' Lynn sang out cynically. 'Well, you were off duty so I hope you told him where he could go.'

After a moment's silence, Julie, her back now to her friend, confessed in a pained voice, 'I almost told him the truth, Lynn. And now I wish I had.'

'What?' Lynn went round the room like a damp squib. 'Tell him the truth and you'll be out on your bottom. Believe me, Julie, St George's is that man's first love. So your playing turned him on? But what happens when you put down the piano lid? I know. On comes Susie.'

FIVE

It was hectic on Eleven. Reception Day and the women to be admitted all standing like refugees in the annex corridor, waiting to be admitted. Also one of the patients had had a heart attack and after an injection of morphia and being given oxygen she had been removed to Intensive Care. This had caused some delay but Sister Grey was again in full control of the situation.

'You had better catheterise the woman in bed three,' she told Julie. 'She's retaining urine and complaining of pain. Check her fluids, Nurse. Make out an Intake and Output chart. Dr Whittaker is going to write her up for something.'

'Yes, Sister.'

'And Nurse Singer...'

Julie turned back again.

'Keep your eye on the patient in bed thirteen. She's rather drowsy this morning. Make sure she's drinking at least two litres.'

Again Julie nodded, then she hurried off to the Sterilising Room to set a catheter tray. She was wondering what had given her such a headache. All morning her head had been thudding and now it was getting worse. She opened up the steriliser and put some catheters into the tray. Eleven on Reception Day was bad enough without added complications. Do this! Do that! No wonder her head was spinning. And at any moment an emergency could arrive. Most likely an abortion. Any one of the five varieties. As Julie set the tray she went over them in her mind: threatened abortion, inevitable, complete, incomplete. And habitual. Good! She'd got them all right. You're learning, she praised herself. Then another wave of nausea straightened her face and this time she wondered if she was sickening for something. Her pulse was going at a frantic rate.

'Nurse Singer!'

Sister again! Julie swung round, guilty.

'Don't stand there waiting for the steriliser,' Sister Grey called impatiently. 'Admit Mrs Kerr to bed ten. And, Nurse, tell Simpson I want her. That auxiliary can never be found.'

'Yes, Sister.' Julie scuttled away down the annex and called out for a Mrs Kerr. 'This way,' she said, giving the woman who stepped up a quick, encouraging smile. 'You're in bed ten, Mrs Kerr.' And, 'Let me take your case.'

'It's all right, Nurse,' the new patient said nervously and clutched at her case fiercely. 'I'm just scared a bit. I've never been in a hospital before.'

Julie glanced at her. The woman was scared; she had broken out into a sweat. 'You'll be all right,' she encouraged again. 'You're next to Mrs Ritchie. You'll like her. And she'll keep you informed.' Drawing the bright, flowered curtain about the bed she then told Mrs Kerr to undress.

'My daughter's with me,' Mrs Kerr said in a wavering voice. 'Could she come in?'

'When you're in bed she can,' Julie advised. 'I want a specimen of urine first, please. There's a glass set up for you in the sluice. That's the room at the bottom of the ward. On your left.'

'Yes, Nurse. Thank you, Nurse. I'll do that.' And with alarm filling her colourless eyes again, she asked, 'How will I know which is my glass?'

'It will have your name on it, Mrs Kerr.' Julie turned down the bedclothes and then asked, 'Will your daughter be able to take your things away?'

'Oh, yes, she'll do that,' the woman asserted.

'Here, let me open your case,' Julie said, as she watched Mrs Kerr's trembling fingers struggle with the lock. 'There we are.'

'I've never been in a hospital before,' the new patient said again.

'You'll be all right,' a high voice shrilled over the curtain. 'Believe me, you'll have

144

had your op before you know where you are. Believe me, they've got a quick turn-over here, Mrs Kerr.'

'Mrs Ritchie,' Julie introduced. 'I told you she'd keep you informed.'

'Has she had her operation?'

'Yes, I've had it,' the voice returned before Julie could answer. 'The day before yesterday and tomorrow I'm getting up.'

'You'll be all right,' Julie said again. Then, hurriedly, she stepped out into the ward again.

Simpson, the auxiliary, was padding up the ward, and Julie told her quickly, 'Sister wants you, Simpson. You'd better hurry up.'

And then David Whittaker appeared in the ward doorway, looking tousled and worn out and still in his theatre clothes. Julie watched him pause to say something to Sister Grey and then off he went again, striding down the annex.

'Nurse Singer!'

Julie's throat worked. What now? She seemed to be the only nurse on the ward.

'Make up a bed,' Sister Grey called authoritatively. 'They've got an emergency in theatre.'

'Yes, Sister.' Dizzily now, Julie wondered what to do first.

'Make the theatre bed up first,' Sister Grey called, seeing Julie's hesitation. 'Then catheterise Mrs Knox. I'll tell Mrs Kerr's daughter she can go in now.'

'I haven't made her charts up yet, Sister,' Julie gulped.

'I'll do that, Nurse...' And as Simpson padded up. 'There's a Mrs Knox in the waiting-room, Simpson. Admit her to bed eleven.'

Julie hurried on to the Sterilising Room, passing Simpson on her way back to the ward.

'Are you all right, Nurse Singer?' Simpson called under her breath. 'You look ghastly.' And, with a grimace, 'Pace too much for you?'

Ignoring the auxiliary, Julie hurried back into the ward. She had a theatre bed to make up. And a woman to catheterise. And her head was spinning. Also Sister was eyeing her with an impatient expression. Oh Lord! She had almost forgotten the urine glass for Mrs Kerr. Back she shot to the Sterilising Room.

At three o'clock the new patients had settled in and the emergency was back from theatre. Now the patients chatted more happily, the old patients giving the new the benefit of their experience. Simpson and Dixon, the junior, were setting the tea-trolley in the kitchen, and Staff Nurse Grey was keeping an eye on the emergency. Julie was in the Sterilising Room, trying to pack drums. But it was becoming more difficult. She felt ill; her head throbbed, she had a pain in her stomach and now the more frightful nausea persisted. Again she leaned forward over a drum, again she closed her eyes.

A step in the doorway made her raise her head and saw to her surprise it was that of Adam.

'Hello,' he said in a tired voice.

'Hello,' Julie whispered.

Adam gave Julie a long, disconcerting stare and then deliberately stepped into the room. And now his stare was penetratingly professional.

'Julie,' he questioned, 'are you all right? You don't look well.'

'I feel sick,' she answered promptly. 'And I've got a headache.'

'Then what are you doing on duty?' His voice was harsh now. 'You look as though you could have a temperature,' he added.

'I think I have,' she echoed bleakly.

'Then off to Sick-Bay, Nurse,' he said sharply. 'I'll tell Sister that I sent you. It may be nothing, but we can't afford to take chances. Not on my ward.'

His ward! That was all he cared about. Glaring back at him, Julie suddenly felt very sorry for herself.

'Go at once,' he ordered, raising his voice a little. 'I'll see you later. At the moment I must look at the emergency.'

'I'd rather go to my room,' Julie began, but he waved her on with, 'Do as I say, Nurse. As I said, we don't take chances. Do you want to start an epidemic?'

She shook her head. 'I'll go,' she said thinly and because she suddenly felt worse.

At the entrance to Sick-Bay Julie almost fainted. The nurse in charge, Sister Potter, a long-limbed young woman who wore rather too much make-up, helped her into the small ward where six spartan-looking beds stood empty.

'So I'm back in business,' she joked. 'What's wrong with you, Nurse?' And when Julie did not answer her, said, 'We'll have you in the bed by the window then.'

'I can't go to bed,' Julie choked. 'I haven't got my gear. Can I go for it, Sister. I need a nightie and my soap-bag.'

Sister Potter shook her head. 'You get into bed,' she asserted. 'I've got a truck-load of nighties. And plenty of soap. We'll see about your own things later.'

'The Prof said he would examine me,'

Julie told Sister Potter in a distressed tone as she sank on to the bed. 'But I'm sure it's just a bilious attack. I used to get them a lot. I wish you would tell him. There's no need for him to bother with me.'

'I'd hardly tell a man like that what to do,' Sister Potter said with a grimace. 'Besides, Nurse,' she added tartly, 'we usually have a doctor to make the diagnosis.'

'I'm sure it's passing off,' Julie began again, still reluctant to take off her clothes. 'I've got a good mind to go.'

'If you don't do as you're told, Nurse, then I will have to give Matron a ring.' Sister Potter warned levelly. 'So be a good girl, take off your clothes, put on this nightgown and get into bed. After that, I'll take your temperature. You look very flushed.'

Julie at last did as she was told, and Sister Potter eyed her soberly as she drew the grey-white institution nightgown over her head and finally got into bed.

'That's better,' she said, more cheerfully, already tidying up the bed. 'Now just you lie there until the Prof arrives. And stick this in your mouth.'

'It's up,' Sister told Julie after a few minutes, and as she shook down the thermometer and then returned it to its holder. 'It's more than a bilious attack, I would say. What have you been eating? Been out on a binge?' And, eyeing Julie again, she added, 'I think it's food poisoning.'

'It's a bilious attack,' Julie returned staunchly. 'I'm used to them. I'd get better just as quickly in my own room.'

Half an hour later the ward door opened and the Prof swung into the room, followed by Sister Potter. His manner was professional, impersonal.

'How do you feel, Nurse?' he enquired as he ran his professional eye over Julie's flushed face, her set mouth, and angry eyes. 'Sick?'

She nodded but would not look at him.

'I'll examine Nurse.' His eyes on Sister Potter, he added lightly, 'Please remove her nightgown.'

'Sit up, Nurse.'

Julie glared into Sister Potter's wide eyes. Then, avoiding the Prof's eyes and shivering violently, she felt the nightgown being drawn from her, leaving her completely exposed. Completely undermined, she kept her eyes on the ceiling and only winced when she felt the cold stethoscope pressed to her skin. She knew that Adam was regarding her objectively, his eyes coldly professional as they ranged over her slight body. He was an expert, well used to watching the rise and fall of a woman's chest. Eyes still on the ceiling, she felt his hands run over her with the precise professionalism, each movement a gesture which told him something, also one which he used quite indifferently a hundred times a day.

'All right, Nurse,' he said at last, after lifting Julie's hair and examining her glands. 'Now open your mouth.'

Trembling, Julie took a deep breath and then opened her mouth. Adam shone his torch into her throat, and then drew back, his eyes momentarily brushing Julie's. And as though her eyes betrayed all he wanted to know he suddenly squared his shoulders and took a deep breath.

'That seems to be all right,' he said, clearing his throat. Then in his usual controlled voice, 'Sister, keep Nurse in bed for a couple of days. Give her plenty of fluids but no solid food. I'll look in again in the morning.'

'Yes, sir.' Sister Potter gave him one of her most radiant smiles and then started for the door.

As she watched them go, Julie thought irritably, so the rumours about Sister Potter were true enough ... the woman had an unquenchable taste for men. Walking ahead of Adam, she positively flirted with her hips. Now she was posturing at the door. Silly bitch! Julie flopped back against her pillows, feeling unreasonably angry. Why, she cursed inwardly, why had Adam to see her in that wretched nightgown? Suddenly she groaned and then sitting up quickly she shouted as loud as she could for a scoop.

After a session with the scoop, Julie began to feel better. She even began to like Sister Potter, for she had been very helpful and sympathetic. 'Thanks, Sister,' she breathed. 'I'm sorry about all that. Isn't there a junior?'

'Yes,' Sister Potter answered brightly, 'there's little Nurse Grey. She comes on at four, so you'll be all right. And stop worrying, Singer. You're a bundle of nerves, aren't you?'

Julie lowered her eyes. She was a bundle of nerves, she felt all to pieces, cornered, and suddenly very vulnerable.

'You're the nurse who plays the piano, aren't you?' Sister Potter went on, hoping for a chat.

Julie nodded.

'You're good,' Sister Potter enthused. 'And I must say I like a bit of the classical myself.'

Julie said, 'I hope the nausea doesn't come on again,' and she lowered her eyelids, firmed her mouth.

'A couple of days fasting and you'll be as right as rain, Nurse,' Sister Potter encouraged. 'Now lie down and try to get some sleep. The Prof said it could well just be a bilious attack, but he's taking no chances. And don't forget, if you want anything, just ring the bell.'

Ten minutes later Sister Potter returned with a jug of lemon and barley and Julie felt well enough to drink a little. 'Thank you, Sister,' she said as she set the glass down on the bedside locker. 'That was wonderful. I'm beginning to feel more like a survivor. But I would be grateful if you would get in touch with my friend, Nurse Graham, and ask her if she'll get the things I need from my room. She's on Women's Medical. And she's on duty now, unless she's at tea.'

'Yes, I'll do that,' Sister Potter agreed. 'But do stop worrying, Nurse Singer. I've told you, we've got plenty of nightgowns.'

That was what Julie was afraid of. 'Yes,' she murmured politely, 'but I would prefer to wear one of my own. And I would like a word with Nurse Graham, if that would be possible.'

'I'm going for tea now,' Sister Potter said thoughtfully. 'I may see your friend. If not, I'll give her ward a ring.'

'Thank you.' Julie raised another quick smile. Really, she thought, Potter was quite decent.

And she also kept her word. Ten minutes later Lynn breezed in. 'What's hit you? I hope I don't get it,' she said all in one breath. 'Sister says it could be enteritis.'

Julie shook her head. 'It's nerves,' she confessed. 'I usually get a bilious attack when I'm feeling a bit over-wrought. I'll be all right in a couple of days. It was the Prof who designated me to Sick-Bay. I expect he's afraid for his patients. He seems to be constantly suspicious of me.'

'Are you feeling any better?' Lynn asked, in a more worried tone. 'The Prof wouldn't send you here for nothing.'

'Once I get this thing off and my own

nightie on, I'll feel a lot better,' Julie said with a grimace. 'Phew! It doesn't half itch!'

'You haven't got a skin complaint, have you?' Lynn asked, and she screwed her eyes up in mock dismay.

'Don't be silly,' Julie shot back, pulling a face. 'I've been sick, that's all. And now I'm okay again. I just want you to gather some of my things for me. My dressing-gown and slippers. My soap bag and make-up.'

'Are you expecting someone?' Lynn's eyebrows rose.

'Just the Prof. He said he'd look in again.'

'He did! Well, Sister Potter will soon have that round. He'll have to unravel you or something just to make his visits authentic. The Prof's not the stomach man.'

'Lynn!' Julie suddenly felt like screaming. 'For goodness sake, stop going on. I'm not in the mood for your banter. I just want you to get my things for me.'

'And a book or two? A couple of stone of grapes?'

Julie gave up. 'One of these days you'll be

off to the funny farm,' she groaned. 'Can't you ever be serious. I'm not on the danger list but I do feel a bit off. I am in Sick-Bay.'

'Okay, I'll see to it.' Lynn drew down her brows, sobered her eyes. And Julie burst out laughing. 'All right,' she groaned again, 'it doesn't suit you. Just be yourself, Lynn. I give up.'

'Want to hear the latest?'

Julie closed her eyes. 'All right but trim it down,' she said with a long sigh.

'That damned porter, Freddy, had the nerve to want to date me. I wouldn't care they say he's always plastered. Talk about giving your ego a boost.'

'What's wrong with him?' Julie murmured, her eye on the scoop again.

'He's not in my league, that's all,' Lynn snapped angrily. 'And I let him know. Yes, I want to improve myself, I said. So what have you to offer?'

'Lynn...' Julie sat forward, her face a ghastly white again.

'Oh, my God! Hold it!' With a frantic

scramble Lynn got the scoop to Julie just in time. Grimacing, she held it while Julie groaned miserably. 'Coo ... I didn't think you were feeling as dreadful as all this,' she sympathised.

'Just go away,' Julie groaned again.

And then the junior, a thin girl with a chirping, consoling manner, came hurrying into the ward and, after taking one look at Julie, she exclaimed, 'You'd better go, Nurse Graham. I'll see to Nurse Singer.'

It was an uncomfortable night for Julie but the next morning she felt surprisingly better and when Adam peered in the doorway she managed to smile and tell him, 'I'm quite sure it was a bilious attack, Professor Rich. I'm used to them. I know all the symptoms.' Then, because he was staring down at her so hard and with such a strange expression, Julie drew up the sheet with an involuntary movement. Surely, she panicked, he's not going to examine me again!

'I managed to sneak by the night nurse,' he told her, and, glancing up again, Julie saw that he was grinning like a boy.

'I brought you my cassette player,' he said in a more thoughtful tone. 'And some of my favourite tapes. I thought they could be therapeutic in your particular case. It could well be a nervous upset, Julie.'

Because he had called her Julie, and because his voice betrayed a genuine concern for her, Julie gave him another quick smile. And this time their eyes met and held and, once again, Julie felt a rush of consternation, for she knew that Adam was not considering her as a patient but as a man considers a woman to whom he is attracted. The interest was there in his eyes, as plainly as a pointer on a clock.

A silence followed while Julie tried to gather her wits and think more practically. She had captivated his interest with her music, she realised this. Without it, she would not be much of a proposition for a man like Adam.

'I'll be out of this bed very soon,' she said in an almost aggressive voice.

Ignoring this display of emotion, Adam sat on the edge of the bed and went on gently. 'I'm sorry our friendship got off to a bad start, Julie. It would seem I do not wield my words as mightily as I do the scalpel. Perhaps I was tactless – but I certainly did not intend to be. But there, it's never too late to correct past mistakes. And I would like to try again. I know how much your music means to you. I admire your devotion to your work, but, Julie, I could help you. I want so much to help you.'

Julie could not speak and, standing up again, Adam Rich looked down at her curiously. Then after sighing he smiled again and told her, 'I'd really like to know what is going on in that talented little head of yours. But there, for the time being, it seems I must wait – at least until you feel better. More communicative.'

'Thank you for bringing the tapes,' Julie said in a small voice. 'You are kind, Adam.'

Julie saw his body brace up confidently at the use of his Christian name, but just at that moment Sister Potter came flurrying into the ward and, politely, the Prof turned to greet her.

'She looks a lot better, doesn't she?' Sister Potter said at once and with deft hands she straightened Julie's pillows.

'You could check Nurse's temperature, Sister.' Adam's smile was disarming and Julie could see the effect it was having on Sister Potter.

'Yes, sir...'

'Thank you, Sister,' Adam went on levelly. 'I think that is all. I don't think we need worry too much about Nurse Singer. Or an epidemic of enteritis.'

'No, sir, I think not,' Sister Potter laughed as she fluttered her eyelids in Adam's direction again. 'Can I get you a coffee, Professor Rich?'

Adam shook his head. 'Thank you all the same, Sister,' he said charmingly, 'but I really must be on my way to Eleven.' Glancing at his watch and then at Julie, he added, 'I will look in again this evening,

Sister. And by that time I'm sure I'll be more than willing to take advantage of your kind offer.'

Through narrowed eyes Julie watched them go. Then there was nothing but the sound of her own heart and the receding footsteps on the corridor outside. She glanced at the file of tapes which Adam had put on her bed-table. And now Julie smiled; she could not stop smiling. In a subtle way, Adam was making himself known to her. For was not a person known by the music they listened to? Julie's throat worked with emotion as she drew up the cassette recorder. After another litre of barley water, she decided, she would lie back and listen to Adam's music. Frowning a little now, Julie's head fell back against her pillows as she thought of Adam. He so obviously saw her as a penniless nurse with a talent he felt morally responsible to promote. If only she could tell him the truth! If only she could say outright, 'Look, I've got to get my SRN, then I can collect a fortune. A fortune which will enable me to get back to my world of music, one which will enable me to provide for my mother and brother.'

Still, Julie considered as she tilted her head thoughtfully, he was kind. Charitable. And he was a brilliant surgeon. And he had been right: she was not destined for a world of blood and sepsis. Her soul had wings. Her talent enabled her to fly, to soar above the mundane things of earth. Smiling again, Julie glanced down at her hands. In her fingertips lay this magic. And for it she would always remember to be grateful.

A step on the corridor outside, and Sister Potter hurried back into the ward.

'That was a surprise,' she called in a friendly tone, and a secretive little smile hovered about her bright lilac lips. 'He's gorgeous, isn't he? I wouldn't mind a little nausea if it would bring the Prof to my bedside.'

'I happen to be one of his nurses,' Julie put in quickly. 'The Prof's not looking after me, Sister. He's looking after Ward Eleven.'

'No doubt, Nurse,' Sister Potter agreed, with another reflective smile. Then in a more businesslike tone she said, 'I'll take your temp Nurse. Then the junior can make your bed. Sorry, no breakfast. But I expect you'll want to go along to the bathroom.'

'Yes, I will,' Julie asserted, and she slid her legs over the edge of the bed. 'I'm beginning to feel a bit of a fraud lying here.' Frowning again, she slid her feet into a very large pair of slippers and then picked up the towel and soap Sister had given her. 'I won't be long,' she said, still grimacing.

When Julie returned to the ward she found that Lynn had been and left a large bundle of clothes on the bed. Also some glossy magazines. Pleased, Julie quickly changed into one of her pretty nightgowns and after brightening herself up with a touch of make-up she then got back into bed.

Then she saw the letter!

It was from the solicitors in New York.

The colour draining from her face, Julie

hastily tore open the envelope, and read,

Dear Miss Singer,

Thank you for Matron's report which we have now received safely. One of your late uncle's beneficiaries, a Mr Herman Brook has asked us for your address as he would very much like to make your acquaintance when he visits England next month. With best wishes,

MIDDLEMASS AND SINCLAIR

Next month! Julie's eyes sought the postmark. It was next month! It was June and the letter had been posted in May. Mr Herman Brook, whoever he was, could arrive any moment. Astonished by this news, Julie sat back, the letter in her hand. And now her eyes grew sober, full of suspicion. Were Middlesmass and Sinclair suspicious? Had they sent this Herman Brook to check up?

'Oh, you're back in bed, Nurse,' Sister Potter called as she breezed back into the

166

ward, carrying a vase of flowers. 'I must say you look better,' she added, her eyes on Julie's nightgown. 'And a letter?'

Potter really was a nosey bitch, thought Julie, as she murmured in a non-committal tone. 'Just someone writing to say an American is coming to see me...'

'An American?' Sister Potter's eyes brightened with interest. 'Who is he?' she enquired. 'What does he do?'

'I couldn't say,' Julie answered honestly. 'I've never met the man.' And changing the subject she went on, 'Would you mind if I played one or two tapes, Sister. The Prof brought them in for me.'

'Not at all,' Sister Potter shrugged, and she rolled her eyes heavenward. 'It seems the Prof has taken over.'

'Not really,' Julie laughed back, self-consciously. 'But he is thoughtful. And kind. And not half as aloof as they make him out to be.'

'He's practically engaged to Dr Tulip, I hear,' Sister Potter laid out. 'Lucky Dr Tulip.'

167

Julie was not to trip into this trap. Sister Potter, she knew to be a renowned gossip. 'Oh, one of the Brandenburg Concertos,' she enthused. 'I must hear this. Do you know the Brandenburg, Sister?'

Again Sister Potter rolled her eyes. She did not. But she did hear the commotion outside in the corridor and at once she squared her shoulders and marched to the door. Julie watched her go, her heart beating violently. It was Dr Tulip's voice she had heard! She was sure of it. But what could Dr Tulip be doing in Sick-Bay? Again, Julie pricked up her ears. Now it was a man's voice that echoed on the corridor. A man with an American accent!

A minute later Sister Potter ushered a very big man into the ward and Julie sat forward in amazement.

'Your American,' Sister Potter laughed. 'He got here almost before your letter.'

Julie stared at him. Herman Brook was big, blond and brash. And one with an eye for the ladies. With an involuntary action, she smoothed her hair and straightened her shoulder-straps. Already his big, blue eyes were all over her. She felt the colour rushing up from her throat, and again, without realising it, she drew up the sheet.

'Well, bless my soul!' Herman Brook's voice filled the ward. 'So you're the little lady. And you're in bed!' Extending a large hand, he clamped it to Julie's and introduced himself with, 'Herman Brook. Close friend of your late uncle's, Miss Julie. I couldn't come all this way without looking you up, now could I?' Dropping her hand to stand back and study her more fully, he frowned now and queried, 'But you're not sick?'

'I was last night,' Julie said in a small, strangled voice, 'but I'm feeling much better now. And I'm pleased to meet you, Mr Brook. It's not visiting time but if Sister doesn't mind.'

'It's quite all right, Nurse,' Sister Potter put in promptly. 'We're not going to turn away someone who has come all the way from the States to see you.'

'Well, bless my soul!' the American exclaimed and he swung round to stare at Sister Potter more objectively. 'Sister, you're a doll,' he said. 'A real, nice doll.'

'Would you like a coffee?' Sister Potter asked, an odd little smile about her mouth.

'I sure would, Sister. That would be nice. Thanks a million.' Swinging a chair under him, Herman beamed again as he suggested, 'What about a coffee for everyone, Sister. Let's make it a party.'

'So early in the morning?' This time Sister Potter exchanged a glance of amusement with Julie, then shrugging her shoulders she hurried out of the ward.

'Quite a doll,' Herman Brook exclaimed, when his glance had returned to Julie. 'Young too.' And now his attitude changed and he stood up, turned his chair round and sat astride it. 'So you're old William's niece,' he sighed. 'And you've had to give up your music to work here just to get his goddam legacy. Well, I'll tell you this, little lady,' he went on, shaking his head in a disapproving manner, 'I never liked the idea. And, what's more, I told your uncle so.'

'You knew my uncle well?' Julie said, staring hard at Herman Brook, and wondering what a big, good-looking, vigorous man of about forty had had in common with her ancient and eccentric uncle. 'I wish I'd known him. I never even saw him. Apparently he fell out with my mum about a hundred years ago.' Pulling a face, she added, 'Over a game of marbles. Can you believe it?'

'I believe it,' Herman grinned. 'I knew the old man. But your uncle wasn't all crazy. He did regret not having made it up with your mother. Remorse weighed heavily on his old shoulders. Most of the time, of course, he was as nutty as hell.'

'Nutty enough to leave his money to someone he had never seen,' Julie said quietly. 'And so you are here to look me over, Mr Herman.'

'Not exactly, young woman,' Herman

Brook asserted and he gave Julie a more thoughtful stare. 'Your old uncle and I were good friends,' he told her and his eyes momentarily clouded with a genuine affection. 'So why shouldn't we be friends?' he grinned again. 'For a start, I want to call you Julie. It's a pretty name. And you're a pretty girl. And I think we are going to spend quite a bit of time together.'

'That would be nice,' Julie agreed.

'And, Julie... To my friends I'm Herman.'

'Okay, Herman.' This time she gave him a quick, amused smile.

'You never know, honey,' he said as he stood up to make way for Sister Potter, who had returned with the coffee tray. 'Herman might help ... I've heard all about you, Julie.'

How, Julie could not imagine, but as they chatted together and Sister Potter and Herman drank their coffee, she began to take more kindly to Herman Brook. He was nice, she decided, when he finally stood up to go. Loud in every conceivable way but still nice.

'Beneath all that brash façade, your Mr Brook is shy of women,' Sister Potter said later.

'And in Tokyo,' Julie tossed back, 'there are no Japs.' Then, she suddenly felt exhausted and, falling back, she closed her eyes and told Sister Potter, 'I think I'll fold up for a while, Sister. I feel a bit weak.'

Julie dozed off but she was awakened again by someone calling, 'Nurse Singer! Nurse Singer!'

Opening her eyes, she caught her breath. It was Dr Susie Tulip! Whatever did she want? As she struggled up and frowned at the woman who had so rudely awakened her, Susie Tulip said,

'You know who I am, Nurse Singer. We have met. And now I would like to talk to you.'

Julie sat forward, aware now of the bright gleam of cunning in the beautiful Susie's eyes. 'What do you want?' she said. 'If the Prof sent you to look me over, I'm much better now, thank you.'

'I have not,' Susie said in a clipped voice, 'come to make a diagnosis, Nurse. I have come to deliver an ultimatum.'

'Ultimatum?' Julie's head jerked back as she met Susie's hard, penetrating eyes. 'Whatever do you mean?' she breathed.

Slowly, each step a threat, Susie Tulip moved to the side of Julie's bed.

'I've been having a chat with your American friend,' she said and she paused to smile slyly at Julie. 'He's quite a character,' she began again, and now there was an air of triumph in her voice. 'And *most* informative.' Another loaded pause and then, 'It seems that you might well become a rich woman one day, Nurse Singer. That is, if you bravely struggle on until you get your SRN. And I will say this, I do agree with Mr Brook as to the proviso made by your late uncle. It was tough. But here you are at St George's, Nurse. On a false pretence, of course – Tut, tut, and Adam was just saying how you enjoyed nursing... How you loved helping other people.'

Smirking mockingly again, Susie stepped back to the foot of the bed and again her eyes blazed fiercely. 'You,' she emphasised, 'are using this fine establishment as a means of laying your hands on a fortune. I wonder what Matron would think about that?'

Shock had stunned Julie. She could only stare dumbly back at Susie Tulip. But at last she managed to falter, 'I refuse to discuss my affairs with you, Dr Tulip. Will you please go.'

'Not until I've said my piece, Nurse,' Susie Tulip laughed back, her eyes flashing dangerously. 'I'm a determined character, too, Nurse Singer. And I happen to be determined to marry Adam without delay. So you take your fortune. And stop trying to seduce a surgeon with your piano-playing. It won't get you anywhere. Unless, of course, it's even more money you want. Adam is a sucker when it comes to lame dogs ... or artists. If you refuse to stop pestering him, then I will make it my business to inform Matron as to your true reason for being here at St George's. Then, Nurse, it would certainly be goodbye to an SRN. And in your case, a fortune. We would certainly see that no other training school accepted you.'

Again, Julie could only stare helplessly back at Susie. So the big American had unwittingly given her away. And now her very future lay in the hands of an unscrupulous woman. And, in love, she knew women could be unscrupulous, capable of deceit, lies – in Susie's case, blackmail.

'Think about it,' Susie said in a soft, lethal tone, then as quietly as a cat she went from the room.

SIX

Julie did think about Dr Tulip's ultimatum; she thought about nothing else for the rest of the morning. Furious, angry, bitter thoughts buzzed madly in her head until the torture and confusion was suddenly too much for her and, jerking up, she sat forward and reached desperately for Adam's cassette player. Always for her music had been the anodyne for all ills. On so many unhappy occasions it had brought sweet calm to a troubled mind and, now again, Julie sank back, her eyes closed as the first soothing strains of music filled the ward. And, magically, within moments, Susie Tulip was forgotten, her outrage quelled, and a faint smile touched Julie's lips as she again found sanctuary in one of her favourite concertos. Again a romantic sadness, notes sweet and poignant, then brilliant and vigorous, seemed to release Julie's very soul. Again, some part of her winged heavenward.

Only though to plummet back to earth with a shock. Now Julie sat forward again, her lips firmly compressed as realisation hardened her eyes. She was listening to a recording of her own playing! Adam had taped her performance with the orchestra in Newcastle. And so, she told herself, she must listen more objectively, critically. There were flaws!

Adam did not look in again until after seven. He was wearing a smart car-coat with a fur collar over a fine beige sweater and he looked pleased; as though he was going somewhere.

'Hello,' he said and he stood contemplating Julie with a professional eye. 'How do you feel now?'

Averting her eyes, Julie thought, I'd like to tell him what I thought about his Susie with thoughts as hot as her scarlet shirt and an intent as black as her trews. Again jealousy nearly overwhelmed Julie but she managed to take a deep breath and say coolly, 'I'm not sick any more. It was a bilious attack.'

'Good! That's splendid!' Amusement flickered in Adam's dark eyes as he tried again to capture Julie's gaze. 'I see you've been playing my tapes,' he said. 'That's a good sign.'

'I listened to the recording you made of the concert,' Julie said in an aggressive tone this time. And, giving him a sharp glance. 'You are not allowed to make recordings of a concert.'

'Perhaps not,' Adam said lightly, shrugging his shoulders, 'but I assure you that I do not intend using this tape for commercial purposes. I recorded that performance for my own private use. As well you know.' Moving back to the foot of the bed he now considered Julie from full vantage and he went on in a more thoughtful tone, 'You seem out of sorts, Julie. I imagined you would enjoy listening to your own playing. I wanted to surprise you, please you. I certainly enjoy listening to it. Indeed, every time I play it I'm even more surprised. Astonished even.' His smile verged on tenderness now as he went on in a lowered tone, 'You continue to amaze me, Julie. I find it difficult to believe.'

'What?' Julie burst out indignantly, her eyes glaring their protest. 'Difficult, I suppose to believe that a mere nurse has imagination, talent. You think we were made to dash about with domestic utensils, make beds.' Breathlessly, carried away by a feeling of aggression she did not understand, Julie continued to rage, 'Perhaps you would like to transplant this talent of mine. You would really like to see Dr Tulip on that concert stage, wouldn't you?'

'My God!' Adam's throat worked as he stood back as though to examine Julie's outburst. Then a puzzled look came into his dark eyes and his voice was sharp, authoritative as he exclaimed, 'You know you are being ridiculous, Julie. Stupid! What has Susie got to do with us?'

US? The word filled Julie with a fresh agitation. Such a small word but it had instantly set her heart thudding violently. Suddenly she wanted Adam more than anything in the world. More than her music, more than a fortune. 'I must have a fever, after all,' she laughed shakily, but still she could not look at him.

'Julie.' Adam returned to the side of the bed and now sat down on the edge of it. 'Us,' he repeated in a gentle, lowered tone. 'You and I, Julie. You know why I'm here.' Smiling, his eyes tender, he reached out to take Julie's hand, to smooth out her fingers. 'Sister Potter, I'm confident, could well see to a case of biliousness,' he teased. 'I'm also confident that you know why I'm continually concerned about you. I do intend to spell it out, but I had hoped for a less inhibiting setting.'

'Tell me what?' Julie's gaze was still hard on the sheet.

A pause and then Adam moved a little

closer to Julie. 'You know what has happened,' he said in a firm voice. 'I've fallen in love with you, Julie.'

Another pause as Julie's throat worked with emotion, as the colour flooded up from her throat, as she raised eyes full of pain.

'I love you, Julie,' Adam said again and this time his warm rich, deep voice washed over Julie like some aphrodisiac sauce. For a moment she felt his hand move along her arm, his fingertips add their message and, though she wanted to look deep into his eyes, she could not look at him at all.

'I had no idea,' she said in a small voice. 'I'm sorry, Adam. I thought it was just my music you were interested in.' She could not go on but in her mind's eye she could see him standing erect, his face like granite, his eyes reflecting the hard discipline of a mind which must never be confused.

'Then there is someone else?'

Julie nodded.

Another bleak silence and then Adam said shortly, 'I understand.'

'An American,' Julie went on dizzily. 'He's here on holiday at the moment. His name is Brook. Herman Brook.'

'I see ... then, Julie, I think I can nicely discharge you. You have the rest of the week off and start your duties again next Monday.'

This time Julie could not trust herself to answer him. She nodded again and then thankfully turned to the doorway through which Sister Potter now came like a galloping emu.

'I'm sorry, sir,' Sister Potter called blithely. 'I didn't know you were here, Professor Rich. The coffee is on, if you want it?'

'No, thank you, Sister,' Adam said in a clipped voice as he started to the door. 'But I have arranged for Nurse Singer's discharge. She's to have the rest of the week off and return to her ward on Monday. It was a bilious attack, nothing worse.'

'Yes, sir.' Bleakly now, Sister Potter followed him out of the ward. And bleakly now, Julie slid down the bed.

She lay in a state of inertia. The whole world had suddenly grown dull. The whole aspect of the Sick-Bay depressed her. Turning to the windows she realised that they had no view at all. Tall, dehydrated-looking buildings encroached oppressively and only one haggard-looking tree rose from the dried-up turf of the courtyard. There was also a nauseating smell of petrol.

With a rush of tears Julie brought the sheet up over her head. If she didn't sleep a wink for a year, she told herself, she must convince herself that she had done the right thing. A fortune! The chance to provide for her mother and brother! Ten years hard slogging at her music! They were not to be thrown aside for the whim of a surgeon. Susie Tulip could well have been right when she had said Adam would never have noticed her had it not been for her piano-playing. With this thought in mind Julie tried desperately to console herself.

The following week, back in the Nurses' Home, Julie got a phone-call from Herman

Brook. He was sure glad to hear that she was well again and he intended to pick her up at two o'clock. For once in her life Julie reached for a cigarette. Then she told Lynn, 'He's a big, loud extrovert, Lynn. A friend of my late uncle's. You'll have to meet him. And this week I'll certainly be glad of his company.'

'Oh!' Lynn frowned suspiciously at Julie. 'Why don't you tell me what's wrong?' she said, to the point.

It took exactly two minutes to tell Lynn what had happened, then she picked up her soap-bag and started to the door. 'So now you know,' she sighed. 'I'm going for a bath. Perhaps you'll be able to come up with something. Susie Tulip's nothing but a moral blackmailer and she shouldn't get away with it.'

'Then why did you let her!' Lynn exclaimed, her small, pert face indignant with shock. 'Do you know, Julie, I sometimes think you're as nutty as hell. Why didn't you laugh in her face. Bluff your way out of it. You should have said, Come on, then Susie, we'll both see Matron.' Pulling a face, Lynn added, 'As for your Mr Brook, he must be a bit of a big mouth.'

'I'm lucky it wasn't Matron he bumped into,' Julie said wryly, and as she hung on the side of the door, 'No, Lynn, I did the right thing.'

'Well, you do want to get your SRN and be a concert pianist,' Lynn rebuked. 'Susie just wants the Prof. Let him go.'

Flinging back the door, Julie hurried out into the corridor. Lynn was right, she couldn't have everything. And she had made a wise decision. She would have been a fool to throw everything away for a man, she again desperately tried to convince herself.

At two o'clock Herman Brook met Julie at the hospital gates. He was wearing an enormous hound's-tooth jacket with a carnation pinned to the lapel. Ghastly, Julie thought, as she gave him a quick smile.

'You look great,' he bellowed, and his protruding eyes ranged over Julie's new denim suit. 'Just great!' And taking Julie's small, cold hand in his podgy, moist one, he quickly led her round the corner to where he had parked his car. 'Now,' he went on in a boyishly pleased tone, 'where shall we go? It's too early for a show. Too late for lunch. What about a jaunt into the countryside. A run up to the Border?'

'That would be nice,' Julie agreed, forcing herself to sound a little enthusiastic. 'I'd like to get the ether out of my lungs.'

'That should help, then. A present for the little lady,' Herman said as he pressed a small parcel on to Julie's lap before settling himself in the driving-seat. 'It's good stuff. I brought it over with me. Honey, that will soon dismiss the ether and any ideas that go with it.'

'Thank you...' Julie raised a smile but she made no attempt to open the package and, as they drove out of town and started on the road to Scotland, she found herself thinking again of Adam. She could not stop thinking of him. With dismay she wondered if he was to haunt her for ever.

'Something on your mind, honey?' Herman enquired, and one podgy hand dropped to Julie's knee.

'Nothing really.' Discreetly she changed her position, turned to the window.

'Hungry, then?'

She shook her head.

'We'll have a drink somewhere,' he persisted. 'Your uncle and I often enjoyed a drink together. He was a hard man. He could take his liquor. And he could play a good game of chess,' Herman added in a happy, reflective tone. 'Yes, the old man enjoyed life. When you're dead, you are dead,' he used to say. 'Life is for the living. Enjoy it, Herman.'

'And no doubt you do,' Julie put in, raising a smile.

As they drove on, Herman went on telling Julie stories about her late uncle, and then they started towards the hills. Rippling little hills, lime-green, crimson and yellow in the sunlight. And, beyond them, Scotland.

'Well, blow me,' Herman exclaimed. 'But where is the heather?'

'You'll not see that until August,' Julie informed. 'That is, if you're still here in England.'

'Maybe I will, maybe I won't. We'll have to see, won't we?' Herman laughed gaily. 'It was old Isaac, your uncle, who used to talk about the Scotch heather.'

'Let's take a walk,' Julie urged. 'Pull in here, Herman. We're on the Border now. Look, there is the sign.'

'Well, bless me!' Herman exclaimed as he brought the car to a standstill and switched off the ignition. 'You're in Scotland now, old fellow!' And, after staring over the wide, undulating fells, he said, 'This is a wild place. Sure you want to walk, Julie?'

'I'm sure,' she said, giving his hand a tug. 'And it would do you good, Herman. Come on.'

'Just as you say, little lady.' Grinning, he heaved himself out of the car and started after Julie along the road to the summit.

Catching her up, he caught her hand again. 'When you've got that goddam certificate,' he began excitedly, 'and you're back in London I can see Herman making more business trips to London. And we'll make the most of them, Julie. You're a nice girl. I like you. Your uncle would have liked you too.'

Stopping to lean against a fence, a wall of conifers behind them, a rolling sea of hills ahead, Herman now slipped his arm across Julie's shoulder. 'I suppose you think I'm an old man,' he began probingly. 'Well, Julie, I am forty, but I've made a packet and you and I could have a great time. Why let a few years spoil things? I think we were destined to meet. Just as I was destined to befriend your old uncle.'

He doesn't like women! Julie thought furiously. It's a disease with him. Brushing off his arm, she forced a laugh and teased, 'I think you should meet my mother, Herman. She's a widow-woman, and very attractive.'

'I won't be put off,' said Herman, and this

time he turned away so that Julie could not see his expression. Had she she would not have taken Herman for such a clown.

Later that evening they went for a meal at a hotel just over the Border and, although Herman ate as greedily as a sultan and drank too much, Julie had to admit she had actually enjoyed their outing. Outside the hospital she even gave herself up to a bear-like hug and when Herman pressed his big, moist mouth to her own, she felt no repugnance. She felt nothing; nothing at all and, as the car glided away, she completely forgot him. Now, her shoulders a little hunched, Julie thought of Adam. Where was he now? And with whom? Susie, of course! They would be making love together. Jealously lashed savagely at Julie. Again her face twisted with pain. She had done the right thing, but she missed him. And God help her, why did her mind keep filling with such images. Images which made her feel faint with unhappiness, outrage.

It was a sense of desperation that kept

Julie away from the piano in the Nurses' sitting-room for the rest of the week. She felt dismal, hollow inside, as though something vital had been taken from her. Then Herman telephoned.

'There's a concert in the city, honey,' he boomed over the phone. 'A bit too highbrow for me, but you'll certainly enjoy it. And after the concert, just to please Herman, we'll come back to the hotel for drinks. And don't worry about a thing, little woman, I'll pick you up, prompt seven.'

Little woman! Julie set down the receiver and then made a face, a long horrible noise in her throat. He sounded so ghastly, but she would enjoy a concert. It could well give her the drive she so desperately needed. The drive to go on. Herman, she told herself, was good for her.

Back on the ward, it pleased Julie to find that the nurses were glad to see her. Even Bella beamed up from the floor she was washing to call, 'Better now, Nurse? That's good. It's nice to see a smile – the rest of the

192

b ... look so b ... blue. And now Sister's on to me. Says I'm getting podgy. Well, she's had it. She's not getting me on to any diet. I look forward too much to my spaghetti and chips.'

'Well, at least you know what you want,' Julie said, and now she was not smiling. She had to report back on duty and so she hurried on into the ward. And stopped dead when she saw that Adam, accompanied by his mob of students, was doing a ward round. Turning, she meant to scurry away, but the shrill voice of Sister Grey calling, 'Nurse Singer!' made her turn back again. She headed up the ward, swallowing hard, smiling here and there at patients who recognised her.

'Yes, Sister.' Deliberately, she kept her eyes from Adam.

'Weren't you going to report back on duty, Nurse?' Sister Grey's voice was sharp.

'I saw you were busy, Sister.'

'We're all busy, Nurse. And there's plenty for you to do. Professor Rich wants to examine the woman in bed sixteen, so would you prepare an examination tray. Then you can do the medicines with Nurse Baron. Nurse Dixon is on her day off, so don't waste any time.'

'Yes, Sister.'

As she turned to go, Julie glimpsed Adam's eyes upon her, hard and remote like those of a jurist. A rush of unhappiness again brought tears to her eyes but she managed to straighten her back, hold up her chin and walk smartly from the ward.

It was in the annex corridor that Julie paused. Why she did so she could not tell. Then she noticed that the door of the side-ward was half open and again something compelled her to push the door open a little farther. Fearfully now, she peered into the room and on to the bed over which a pale ray of sunlight spread.

Hesitantly, Julie took another step into the room, but now her eyes were fixed on the bed and the patient who lay on it. And she could not take her eyes from her, she could not stop staring.

'She looks a bit odd, doesn't she?' a familiar voice said behind her and springing round fearfully, Julie looked into Bella's big, horror-filled eyes.

'I'd take a closer look if I were you, Nurse,' Bella said in an undertone and giving the patient, prone and still, another long look. 'Go on.'

Julie thought her heart was going to burst. There was no need for her to look again; she knew the woman on the bed was dead. She had known it outside in the annex, before she had even seen her. She moved to the foot of the bed and stared bleakly at the stiff, wan face, the dropped jaw and, as she stood there, moisture broke out on Julie's brow and she clenched her hands so tightly that her fingernails cut into her palms. It was her first experience of death and now a certain realisation came to her. Death was real. It was a tangible thing. It was all about her, she felt it, it clung to her. She wanted to run away but she could not. She wanted to say something to Bella, but she could not.

'You'd better tell Sister,' Bella said.

'What is it, Nurse?' Impatiently, Sister Grey turned to Julie again. And because Julie just went on staring at her, 'Nurse, what is it? Is there something wrong?'

Conscious of Adam's eyes on her again, Julie nodded. 'Yes, Sister,' she said in a voice that was barely audible. 'It's the patient in the side-ward. She's dead!'

Sister Grey gave Julie a long look, then, turning abruptly, she headed out of the ward. And now, helplessly, Julie turned to Adam. 'She's dead,' she whispered, only one image in her head now. 'She's dead,' she said again, tremulously. And suddenly she could not stop shaking.

Julie was sure she would have gone to pieces had it not been for Adam's steadying hand on her arm, the lightning concern in his dark eyes. But now he was commanding, 'Nurse, pull yourself together. The patient's mother is in the Day Room and I must break the news to her. You could help by making a pot of tea. She'll certainly need one.'

And then Sister Grey appeared again, her eyes steady as she paused to say something to Adam. Julie turned to the students but they were all filing away. Again she tried to move and found she could not; shock had rooted her to the floor. Sister Grey was calling to her again, and still she could not move.

'Nurse,' Sister Grey said more gently, and, as she eyed Julie more thoughtfully, went on, 'there was nothing we could do for that poor woman. And, believe me, death can sometimes be a miracle in itself. Now the Prof asked you to make a pot of tea, so off you go. And tell Nurse Baron I want a word with her.'

A few kind words and Julie's feet came away from the floor like treacle. She gave Sister Grey a quick, grateful smile and then fled for the sanctuary of the kitchen and the familiar normality of Bella.

'I've got it made,' Bella said the moment

Julie appeared, and she gave the pot another stir. 'And I've poured a cup out for you, Nurse.' Bella added in a motherly tone. 'Go on, have a few mouthfuls.'

That night Julie was more than glad of Herman's lack of enthusiasm over hospital affairs and, after a quick drink at one of the hotels in town, they made their way to the concert hall. Ward Eleven forgotten, Julie took her seat in the stalls and sat back, ready to enjoy herself. And then, just as she turned to hear what Herman was saying her attention was drawn to a man and woman making their way along their rows of seats. And at once, Julie's heart turned over. Adam! And with him Susie Tulip! And Susie looked even more seductive in a black, lush and lacy dress. Julie's throat worked. Desperately, she drew her eyes from Adam, Adam even more attractive in a dark suit and evening shirt. Lean, handsome and masterly, also a perfect foil for the blonde Susie. And any moment they would be face to face, his thighs brushing her own. Her colour draining away, Julie closed her eyes, but even then she was conscious of his warm, hard, virile presence.

'Good evening,' a deep voice said throatily. 'Sorry to trouble you, Nurse.'

Julie stood stiffly, suffocatingly aware of his closeness, acutely embarrassed as he paused to stare directly into her startled eyes.

And now Susie Tulip! She also paused before Julie but it was only to give her an almost rude, curious stare. 'Hello,' she mumbled, before she moved on.

'Hello there!' Julie heard Herman boom. 'Hello there, Dr Tulip. Well, fancy seeing you...' And, peering along the row after Susie with an obvious fascination, 'What about a drink later, baby? During the interval.'

Julie sank back, bitterness in her blue eyes, glad now that the house lights were dimming and the concert about to begin. Suddenly she hated the extrovert at her side, she hated his loud habits and mannerisms. Even now Herman was pressing an enormous box of chocolates into her hands, and murmuring something about a drink they would all have together. Susie impressed him! She was cute! Again he leant forward to beam along the row.

Julie sat back stiffly, wondering if Herman would get so bored that he would doze off. She hoped not because she was sure he was a snorer. God was merciful, Herman did not snore but, hearing the second movement of the concerto, he started to noisily open his box of chocolates. Julie felt her blood drain away with shame. She glared at Herman but he merely grinned back at her and shoved the box in her face.

It was intolerable, Julie decided and making the decision, she stood up quickly. 'I've got a headache,' she muttered under her breath. 'Let's go.'

Outside in the foyer, Herman exclaimed, 'Why didn't you say? We could have gone straight to the hotel. I'm not a quack but I'll soon fix you something to clear that headache. Just leave it to Herman.' And, glancing round the silent foyer, he added with a loud contempt, 'Yeah, let's get out of this goddam funeral parlour.'

'I'll sit here a minute,' Julie said as she sank down on to one of the sofas covered in a wine-coloured velvet. 'You go get the car,' she added in a small voice, having it in mind to escape. 'I must go to the ladies' room.'

There was no time for escape. Glancing up, Julie was amazed to see the door to the concert hall open and Adam come slowly out into the foyer. She held her breath as once again his solemn eyes met her own with a jurist's enquiry.

They stared at each other for a few moments, then Adam came forward slowly, deliberately, and stopping in front of Julie he said in a cool, controlled voice, 'I can guess what ailed you, Julie. Where is he ... this American boyfriend of yours?'

Bracing up a little dignity, Julie retorted, 'I don't know what you mean? I have a head-ache and so Herman has gone for the car.'

'Then you're not having fun?' The dark eyes flickered with amusement but his lips remained cold and drawn.

Again, Julie looked up at Adam in surprise, aware of his mockery, but with no words to defend herself. 'Are you having fun?' she lashed out suddenly, his scrutiny too much to bear. 'Why did you follow me out?'

'I did follow you out, Julie,' he went on levelly. 'Ostensibly, I withdrew. Watching you I came to the conclusion that you could – need a doctor.'

She saw the amusement in his eyes and instantly the colour flooded up to her face. She averted her eyes. She did need a doctor! She needed him! Every nerve of her body screamed out this truth. 'Herman won't be long,' she told him tremulously. 'You're missing the best part of the concerto. Why don't you go back?'

Ignoring her words he said calmly, 'I hear your American is very wealthy. And I can see he's disgustingly healthy.'

Matching his taunt with her own, Julie let fly. 'He's made a bundle. And he's fun. He's not a serious man.'

'Is that why you're laughing?' Adam put in ironically.

Their eyes met and held again and this time Julie was agonisingly conscious of both the flame and the anger within Adam's. She turned away from him, unnerved, shattered by what she had seen in his eyes, shattered also by the power of her own feelings for him.

'You left the hall because Herman Brook was embarrassing you.' Adam made this statement slowly and deliberately and now he calmly took a cigar from a case and lit it.

'Herman does not understand music,' she defended hotly.

'He obviously understands women, I'd say he was forty, warm and willing.'

His words were meant as an insult and Julie shook with fury and began to tremble visibly again. 'I can teach him to love music,' she said.

'A gift of love, indeed!'

Julie stared back at Adam now, startled by his belligerent tone, the dark eyes suddenly hard and accusing. And, although every nerve and fibre of her body urged her on – to fling herself into his arms and confess all – she summoned up her strength and took a step away from him.

Again their eyes met in battle, in entreaty, then Adam inhaled deeply from his cigar and slowly, deliberately, he breathed out a great plume of blue smoke which set up a barrier between them.

A loud breathing and blustering announced Herman's return and, thankfully, Julie turned to the entrance. He had the car key raised in one hand and he was beaming.

Without a word of farewell for Adam, Julie ran to Herman, glad to escape into the night and the waiting car.

Herman had a suite of rooms at the best hotel in town and, very soon, Julie was doing her best to look at ease in his small but pleasant lounge. She watched him fixing a drink for her and she even gave him a smile but she knew she had come to the end of her tether where Herman was concerned, for his lack of tact, his insensitivity, his loud manner and his continual thirst were beginning to unnerve her. Also she did not care for the idea of being in his private suite.

'I mustn't stay very long,' she said as Herman pressed a glass into her hand. 'I'm on duty first thing in the morning and I have a lecture tomorrow night.'

'Oh, forget about it,' Herman said in a reproving tone. 'There's never a tomorrow, Julie, so let's make the most of today. How do you feel?'

'A little better,' Julie answered. 'I'm sorry about the concert, but, truly, my head was ghastly. I could never have concentrated.'

'What was there to concentrate on, honey?' Herman grinned. 'I thought you just sat back and listened.'

Julie stared down at her rich, brown wine and immediately thought of Adam again. Adam would have understood, he could never have made such a remark. But she forced a smile and asked, 'Well, aren't you going to have a drink, Herman?'

'I am, and then I'm going to sit down right beside you, honey.' And pouring out a drink, he then set it down on the table nearby. 'Move along, honey,' he said, staring down at Julie with bright, focused eyes. 'There's plenty of room for us both.'

Julie made a shuffling motion and glanced doubtfully at the small black leather settee but Herman ignored this and set about squeezing his great bulk into the space alongside her, one arm about her shoulder, the other within reaching distance of his glass.

'This is nice,' he breathed heavily against Julie's cheek. 'And at any moment, honey, we'll have our own music. Herman thinks of everything.'

He certainly did, for within moments, the throb of a sexy beat filled the small dimly lighted room and Julie turned to stare at him in dismay. 'What's so funny?' she asked in a hard voice, certain now that she had done the wrong thing in coming to Herman's suite.

'I'm smiling because I'm pleased,' Herman murmured and his fingers began to knead through the soft, lacy sleeves of Julie's dress. 'Aren't you pleased, Julie?'

He had set down his glass and Julie knew that she was trapped. Her face turned scarlet and she turned desperately to reach for her own glass, her only weapon of defence.

Too late, Herman leaned forward and trapped her with his arm and she was forced to fall back. Her throat worked, in dismay she stared at him.

'Come on, honey, just a little kiss. We're going to see a lot of each other in future, Julie. And Herman may just be able to help. I just can't see my little Julie making it in the world of carbolic.'

'I must go, Herman,' Julie's eyes widened in desperation, anger. 'Please, my dress.'

'Damn your dress!' There was a different

light in Herman's eyes now. 'I'll buy you ten to replace it. Julie, you must know how I feel about you.'

Fear rolled into a big hard lump in Julie's throat, her eyes filled with terror. Herman Brook was a strong, virile man and in this mood a determined one. 'I'm sorry,' she faltered. 'I can't...'

Herman was determined she would. Suddenly he was pushing Julie back and gasping ridiculous endearments, his big hands running all over her in caresses so vulgar that she cried out in shame. She struggled for half a minute, she beat at his chest furiously, but it was of no avail, for Herman's mouth had found her own and with a down-drive which paralysed Julie with loathing, he held her.

Later that night Julie told Lynn all about it.

'Then what did you do?' Lynn gasped in horror. 'How did you escape?'

'There was a sound on the corridor outside the door,' Julie breathed, still shocked from her experience. 'Herman glanced up and I let out the most terrible cry. Then I screamed. After that he floundered up and begged me to shut up. I gave a good show of hysteria.'

'You bitch!' Lynn began to laugh, then her expression changed and she sighed and said, 'I've been moved to Men's Surgical, Julie. And it's foul. Quite honestly, I'm getting a bit fed up with nursing. I'd like a change.'

'We could well be going out the door together,' Julie said wryly. 'I'm beginning to feel the same way myself.'

* * * *

The following evening Julie made her way along the main hospital corridor to the Lecture Hall. The nurses ahead of her were laughing and chatting, but there was no smile on Julie's face. She was tired. Theatre Day on Eleven, it had again been hectic. And now, as though she had not had enough of the complications of women's reproduction organs, she was going to a lecture on the subject. Nurse Baron, Eleven's theatre nurse, caught her up and fell in step alongside her, but they walked in silence, Nurse Baron being of the same mind. It wasn't until they were filing into their seats that Nurse Baron nudged Julie and said under her breath, 'The Prof's lecturing. It's a wonder he can stand on his feet after Eleven's list.'

Julie turned pale. She had not realised that Adam was lecturing.

'Did you hear what I said, Singer?' Nurse Baron asserted. 'It's the Prof! Well, at least he gives the nurses a lift. He is gorgeous! Just look at them all getting ready to swoon.'

Julie forced a grin and then sat down next to Baron. 'Thank goodness, we've got in the back row,' she whispered, 'I'll be able to close my eyes.'

'I wouldn't try it,' Nurse Baron advised warningly, but Julie did not hear her. Adam had swung in through the double doors.

Julie held her breath as did every other nurse in the hall, then as Adam squared his shoulders and cleared his throat she lowered her eyes.

'Nurses,' he began in his deep, ribbed velvet voice, and a respectful hush filled the hall. 'Tonight we will go over the physiology of the female reproductive tract. The ovaries for about twelve years of life in a temperate climate...'

A nudge started Julie.

'Take a look at liberated Lil,' Nurse Baron tittered under her breath and her eyes went to one of the nurses, 'I'd like to take that smug look off her face. I almost wish some bloke would do her an injury.'

Not a muscle of Julie's face moved, fatigue came in wave after wave as she turned away from Nurse Baron and fixed her eyes on Adam again. His voice was so deep, so rich, so sonorous. It made her want to cry her heart out. She sat back, closed her eyes again, until the voice was softly droning. And now Julie smiled. She could hear music, she felt it stirring in her brain. Wisps of melodies came into her mind ... then very soon a full orchestra.

'Nurse Singer!'

Blinking her eyes into focus, Julie sat up. The Lecture Hall was empty, the nurses gone. The lecture over. She gave Adam a startled look, then slumped back helplessly. 'I must have fallen asleep,' she told him. 'But it wasn't my fault.'

'I didn't say it was, Julie.' His eyes held Julie's steadily as he went on, 'I just wondered if you were all right.'

A silence fell between them and she waited for him to say something else. She felt trapped, her white stiff apron as inhibiting as a shroud.

'It seems I can't help wondering about you, Julie,' Adam went on gently, his eyes tender. 'I find myself continually concerned for you. What have you been doing?' A pause and then, 'It's hard to believe you prefer that loud-mouth bear to myself.'

'Please Adam!' Tempted, Julie again

looked into his eyes.

'Julie?' His voice dropped to gentle enquiry.

'He's rich and kind and he...' Julie could not go on. With a little groan she fell against Adam. 'He's dreadful!' she confessed. 'I can't bear him! But Dr Tulip wants you, Adam. She *blackmailed* me into not seeing you again. I don't care now because I want you – I don't want a legacy – I love you, Adam.'

'Blackmail! A legacy!' The grimness about his mouth and the twitching of a muscle in his cheek made Julie fall back in dismay.

'Julie,' he went on levelly, his eyes suddenly fierce, 'be careful what you say about Dr Tulip.'

'I will not,' Julie burst out emotionally, 'I want you to know the truth. Dr Tulip threatened me. It was moral blackmail. If I did not steer clear of you, Adam, she said she would inform both you and Matron as to the true reason for my being here at St George's.'

Adam was breathing deeply. 'The true reason?' he queried and his eyes narrowed.

'Yes,' Julie pressed, though cautioned again by the gleam which had appeared in Adam's eyes. 'Herman, the American, informed Dr Tulip. He was one of my late uncle's beneficiaries. And he knew that I could not get the money my uncle left me until I had an SRN. That was a proviso. So now, Adam, you know why I was so determined to stay at St George's. I needed that money. I needed it for my mother and brother. That legacy was going to give me the chance to return to my music. But, Adam, I don't want it now. I only want you. I love you.'

Julie's voice faded as Adam continued to stare at her, his face stiff with consternation and anger, his eyes as black as bullets and just as dangerous. 'So, Nurse,' he said in a voice that would have chilled an eskimo, 'you are not here because you enjoy helping people? Nor because you love nursing?' Again his eyes stripped Julie of all confidence. 'You are here,' he went on and his voice rose with sarcasm, 'to collect. And what's more, you damned well had the nerve to ask for my help–'

'Adam!' Julie's eyes brimmed with entreaty, but already he had turned to go. 'Adam,' she called again, desperately.

'Oh, there you are, darling,' a voice echoed confidently through the empty Lecture Hall. 'I wondered what was keeping you.' Coming forward lightly, Susie Tulip gave Adam a long kiss.

Taking her by the hand, but still glaring at Julie, Adam said, 'Let's go, there is nothing to keep me here now. It's over.'

SEVEN

Lynn had marched happily out of St George's, leaving Julie to do the right thing and work a month's notice. A bitter month for Julie, one in which she suffered the agony of Adam's aloof uninterest, although, she had, more than once, raised her head to see him considering her with a frowning intensity which had instantly disturbed the rhythm of her heart.

But now it was September and both girls were installed in a flat near Bromley and only a few miles from the small hospital for geriatrics, where they had both found work. Julie loathed the work, but she liked the flat. Indeed their good fortune in getting such a place still astounded her. And with a piano! It was difficult to believe, and now with something like suspicion in her eyes Julie considered Lynn across the breakfast table.

'I'll say it again,' Julie said, 'I don't believe we get all this for a fiver. If you are paying more than your share so that I can practise my music, then I really must do full-time at the hospital, Lynn.'

'I'm not a charitable institution,' Lynn snapped back, and she spread her toast thickly with marmalade, as though to demonstrate her point. 'Part-time on geriatrics is enough for you, Julie. You've got to practice, get more engagements. You never know, you may get back to the London College. Something could turn up.'

'It won't be a legacy,' Julie said in a lowered voice. 'I haven't heard from those solicitors again. What do you think they'll do with the money?'

'Keep it,' Lynn sighed. 'Solicitors are never short of a bob or two.'

'Then the sooner I get used to working for my living the better,' Julie said determinedly.

'You know you can't keep away from that

piano,' Lynn battled on. 'Just you forget about the rent, Julie. It's a fiver all right. The bloke that owns it is a friend of mine. We could, of course, be chucked out, but we'll not cross that bridge until we come to it.'

Convinced, Julie sat back to drink her tea. 'You know,' she began again, 'I really admire you, Lynn. I think it's wonderful the way you cheer those old dears. They positively love you. And that's worth more than any certificate.'

'Do you prefer Gyny?' Lynn enquired lightly.

'Not really,' Julie answered reflectively. 'I really did enjoy being on Ward Eleven. It was hectic but I was getting useful. Sister Grey actually said she was sorry I was going.'

'I don't mind the old dears,' Lynn chirped. 'I get a welcome when I trot on to the ward. And, quite honestly, Julie, I loathed surgery. You got some laughs, of course. Remember that fool I told you about? The one who chalked up above his bed, "If you want them removed, get the doctor to do it" and hung his bag of gallstones below it. I won't forget him, but I still hated all those drips and wires and pipes and tubes. I felt like a plumber's mate. No, I'm quite happy. I don't even mind rubbing through a couple of nighties for Mrs Thingy – I can never remember her name. I do though remember that she hasn't a soul in this world.'

'And now she's found you,' Julie capped affectionately. 'Lucky Mrs Thingy.' Then she changed her tone, and her expression and enquired, 'Were you very late last night, Lynn? I didn't hear you come in. Anyone special? Or did you come home – empty-handed?'

Lynn shook her head, but not before Julie had caught her expression, an expression that made her stare at her friend more intently, an expression that made her wonder if she had inadvertently stumbled on some secret. Moistening her lips, she sat back to consider her friend more objectively. Yes, Lynn did look different; just a little furtive, a little self-conscious.

'Don't tell me you've fallen for some guy?' Julie challenged. 'I thought you liked to keep a squad on the go?'

This time Lynn sat back to stare at Julie. 'I'm a liberated woman,' she said smartly. 'I don't intend to give up my freedom for any man. I like a good time, Julie. And I get one because I use my head.'

Julie's eyes narrowed, then she smiled broadly. 'Somehow I get the impression that you are not exactly telling the truth. You've got something rather special going, haven't you? I can tell. Is he someone you've met on the Tube?'

Lynn grinned and stood up. 'Well,' she confessed with a laugh, 'I suppose there is something rather special about this guy. But I must go, Julie. I'm late already.' Reaching the door, Lynn grabbed her coat and tote-bag and glancing back called cheerily, 'Good luck tonight, Julie. You have an engagement, haven't you?'

Julie nodded. 'A modest affair,' she

answered. 'At the Community Centre.'

'Good luck, then,' Lynn called again. 'I'll get out before you start hammering. And don't make anything for me. I'll either scrounge some supper on the ward or call in at the chippy.'

Listening to the receding tap of Lynn's footsteps on the stairs, Julie was still of the belief that her friend was keeping something back. At St George's, Lynn had never been able to keep anything to herself, often embarrassing her with the details of a night out with one of the medics or some other fellow she had picked up. And now this reserve? This silence? And needless aggression? Yes, Julie decided, as she stood up to clear away the breakfast dishes, Lynn had something going. Had she actually fallen in love? She did not think so. Lynn had her own philosophy. Long ago Lynn had decided to lose neither her heart nor her head to any man. She had no desire for fireside sanctuary. If she ever married, Lynn had smacked, it would be for money.

Stacking the dishes, Julie again wondered about their generous landlord. An old friend of Lynn's? Or a new one? A rush of water from the tap dismissed this conjecture and now Julie began to think about the concert and what she should wear. A public concert arranged by the County Librarians, and to be held in the Community Hall. After a few moments Julie decided on something not too formal; her flame taffeta skirt and a black silk shirt to match her boots. She was only one of three artists invited to play. Also there was to be a short talk on the life of the professional musician. She was quite looking forward to the evening.

If only she could stop thinking about Adam Rich! She had done the right thing. She could never have stayed at St George's, working close to Adam, knowing the effect he had upon her. Nor could she have suffered his contempt. Also, for Lynn's sake, she had made the decision. Lynn *had* forged a document, one which, thankfully, would now have been discarded, for she had given up the idea of ever obtaining the legacy. She had, in fact, written to the solicitors informing them of her decision not to go on with her training. So far there had been no reply to her letter.

And she would get over Adam, Julie fought to reassure herself. Hadn't Lynn told her, 'It's a mild dose of delirium tremens, that's all. It will pass.'

★ ★ ★ ★

That evening Julie walked on to the small stage, bowed to the audience, which consisted of some rather snobby-looking, middle-aged women and a few bald-headed gentlemen getting ready to doze in their seats. Then she smiled briefly at her fellow artists, who sat rather glumly to one side of the piano; an older man with a face as long as his cello and a small gnome of a man hugging his violin.

It was as she sat down to play that she got a glimpse of the young man who had obviously wandered into the wrong hall. He was about twenty-three and he had bright, merry eyes and a great mane of copper hair. He wore a denim suit and even from a distance Julie could see the glint of his single ear-ring. Watching him sit down Julie had to smile to herself.

She had decided to play something romantic, a short piece by Delius. And very soon Julie gave herself up to her music. Now the audience, the waiting artists, the music critic from the local paper, who sat in the front row, and the trendy young man were forgotten as once again her soul found enchantment. Even so, Julie's secret world was not closed to Adam and as she played he was there with her and her heart welled up with love for him, and when the melody finally dwindled to a close there were tears in Julie's eyes, also an ache of longing in her slim throat. And, unheeding of the applause, Julie went, almost too quickly, from the stage.

She could not stay and she crept away the

moment she decently could do so. When she stepped out on to the street she was startled by the voice of a young man saying, 'That was great! A highly professional performance, Nurse Singer. And, thank God, there was no maniac to spoil it this time.'

In astonishment, Julie stared at him. The trendy fellow she had noticed in the hall. 'You know me?' she gulped.

'I was at St George's,' he grinned. 'I qualified last month and now I've got a job at Bromley Hospital. I happened to see your name up on the poster in the library, so I had to come along. And it was worth the effort. You played brilliantly.' Grinning again, he said, 'I think we should celebrate. My name is Peter Steel.'

'Celebrate?' Julie swallowed hard, again she stared back at him in consternation.

'What I really mean is, will you have a drink with me?'

His brown eyes were so impish, his smile so charming, Julie could do nothing but smile back at him and say, 'That would be nice. I could do with a drink. I don't remember your face, but if you were at St George's then we're not exactly strangers.'

Peter Steel smiled again, revealing large white teeth. 'There's a cosy place round the corner,' he said, as he took Julie's arm and steered her on. 'Let's go.'

As Julie fell in step alongside him her heart began to beat fast. She had no interest whatever in this Peter Steel but she was hungry for news of St George's. Of Adam! And it was with a feeling of excitement that she followed Peter into the small lounge of a rather posh-looking hotel.

'Actually,' he began, the moment he set their drinks down on the table, and sat down himself to stare at Julie, 'I have a proposition to make to you, Julie. You see, it's like this. A few of my pals, professional chaps, have a group going, but we want it to be different. And someone came up with the idea of having a classical backing. Say someone like you. And perhaps a violinist. We'd give you the extra bounce, of course.'

Julie's lips firmed. So this Peter Steel was actually looking to his own interests. Coolly she said, 'You look young to be qualified.'

'Not really,' he put in quickly, 'I am twenty-four. I intend to specialise. I'm interested in the kids. I want to be a paediatrician.'

'That's nice,' Julie said, interested again, 'I think you look like a paediatrician.' With a giggle she added, 'I can't see you as a gynaecologist. You know, with a carnation in the lapel of your expensive suit.'

He grinned and squeezed his eyelids in mock dismay. 'Nor can I,' he agreed. 'But I would like to be rich. And gynaecologists do make money. Especially if they own private nursing homes. But we won't talk shop, Julie. I'd like to tell you about this group. You could be on to a good thing.'

'Could I?' Julie did not think so. 'I've never had it in mind to be a pop star,' she told him smartly. 'Even one with an electric backing.' Smiling, she went on purposefully, 'I'd even say I was more interested in gynaecology. I used to work on Ward Eleven. Professor Rich's unit.'

'Rich!' Peter Steel sat back to grin reflectively. 'That chap didn't know what was good for him either. Struggling on with his conscience when he could have made a bomb. I'd say he had a brainstorm. All in one week he threw up his job. And ditched his girl. You might remember, he was engaged to Dr Tulip. Some lady to throw over! Her folks are loaded. The Prof could have had his private nursing home in no time. Now he's going to do research. In Boston.' And with a sad shake of his head. 'He had it going for him and he chucked it away.'

Julie leapt up as though someone had just plugged in her seat and she did not stop until she was outside on the street. Luckily, the first bus she saw was going her way and, springing on to it, she just had time to glance back to see Peter Steel waving frantically to her.

It was after ten and the light was on in the

flat. Breathlessly, she burst in upon Lynn, who was relaxing on their small settee, her legs in the air, a magazine in her hands.

'It's all over, then,' said Lynn, glancing up. 'And I can see by your face that all went well.'

'An idiot who trained at St George's was there,' Julie gasped as she flung off her coat. 'He picked me up. We went for a drink. And guess what?'

'You're seeing him again?'

'No way – but he did have news.'

'News?' Lynn's big amber eyes met Julie's.

'Lynn,' Julie burst out. 'Adam is no longer engaged to Susie Tulip. And he's leaving St George's. He's going to America.'

'Good. Then perhaps you'll forget him.' Lynn's eyes lowered to her magazine again.

Flopping down on a chair, Julie suddenly covered her face with her hands. 'Oh, Lynn,' she said brokenly. 'This news has shattered me. I'll never see him again.'

'You look as though you could do with a pint,' Lynn said, eyeing her friend. 'A pint of blood. But never mind, I've got the next best thing. A corpse reviver. Sit still and I'll get you a highball.'

A minute later Lynn set a glass down on the small table beside Julie. 'There!' she said. 'That will do you more good than a temperance cocktail. You can have your milky tea later. Drink that, Julie. You look as though you could do with it.'

Julie held the glass in her hands, and her gaze went to the television and the ashtray on top of it. 'Why I should get into such a state, I don't know,' she confessed meekly. 'He's going to America. He may as well go to the moon!' Turning her eyes to Lynn again, she confessed, 'When I heard he was no longer going to marry Susie,' Julie could not go on for a few moments, then she said, 'Oh, Lynn, what a fool I am. I don't suppose he's given me a thought.'

'Then for the time being put him out of your mind,' Lynn said impatiently. 'He's going to America. So what? He'll be back. You may even meet up again, but for the time being, please don't go into a decline. Because I also have a breaking-point.'

'Sorry, Lynn.' Julie smiled over her glass. 'And thanks. I do feel better.' Her gaze going to the ashtray again, she enquired lightly, 'And what about you? I see you've been entertaining.'

'Yes,' Lynn answered, averting her eyes. 'A friend did call in. Not a dishy type. But nice.' Rolling her eyes, she added, 'And rich. A rich extrovert. Very vulgar.'

'It's funny, isn't it,' Julie went on again, 'but that will of my uncle's has done nothing but fill my life with confusion. I'll never get that legacy and I'll never be a real concert pianist.' Her throat working, Julie muttered, 'And I'll never love anyone but Adam. I can never forget him. And the fact that, had I not been a cheat, I could have had him. He would have helped me to get back to the London College of Music, Lynn. He offered to help. And I threw his offer back in his face. I wanted more!'

'Oh, come on,' Lynn grinned back.

'You've been out all night playing for a snobby mob. And what for? A fiver? Do you call that greedy?'

Julie smiled. 'How's that for fame?' she sighed.

'You are in a bad way,' Lynn went on. 'Have another drink and then go to bed. In the morning light everything will be different.'

'I'm on duty in the morning,' Julie flashed back reassuringly. 'Oh, Lynn, I loathe nursing geriatrics. I can't help it. I must be honest. I hate Sister too. She's like the Mad ruddy Hatter. Got her eye on the clock all the time. She doesn't give the nurses time to breathe. As for the poor patients! They're off for another dip before they're dry from the last one. And they call it a residential home for gentlefolk! You wouldn't be washing Mrs Thingy's nightie if it was.'

'So you don't like geriatrics,' Lynn said. 'I get the message. And here is one for you, I almost forgot to tell you.' Springing round, Lynn picked a letter up from the television

233

top and handed it to Julie. 'For you,' she beamed. 'It came this afternoon. And it looks as though it's from your agent. You're getting known, Julie.'

Yes, it was from her agent. Julie stared at the envelope.

'Go on,' Lynn urged. 'Open it. They might want you for the Wigmore Hall.'

'Hardly,' Julie smirked. 'I've got some hard training ahead before I'm up to that standard.'

'What does it say?' Lynn danced from one foot to another as she watched Julie tear open the envelope.

'I should think they want ten per cent of my fiver,' Julie said grimly, but now as her eyes ran over the notepaper, the colour began to rise up from her throat. 'Well,' she burst out breathlessly. 'I'm getting known. Oh, Lynn, I can hardly believe it. Remember that orchestra I played with in Newcastle? Well, the conductor has especially asked for me. He wants me to play with them again. In Newcastle!'

'Great!' Lynn smacked. 'What did I tell you!'

'And Lynn!' Julie rushed on excitedly. 'They have offered me a fee. A real fee. Not peanuts this time.'

'Answer immediately,' Lynn said in her practical manner. 'I'll get a pen.'

'Lynn!'

Something in Julie's tone, made Lynn turn back.

'I'm not going to play in Newcastle, Lynn,' Julie said in a strangled voice. 'I can't accept this engagement.' With pained eyes, she turned away. 'I'm flattered, of course. But I'm not going. I couldn't.'

'Couldn't? Why not?' Lynn's mouth dropped open.

Julie did not answer at once but when she did it was as though she was talking to herself and not her friend. 'I don't suppose he would be there,' she said in a choked voice, 'but if he did happen to be, then I'd go to pieces. And I'm not taking that chance.'

Lynn's eyes narrowed. 'You must be mad!' she almost shrieked. 'Sick with sentiment. And for a man who is more interested in – in gollop. My God, Julie, how can you be so dumb?'

'I don't know,' Julie said in a faraway voice. 'But it seems I am. I'm not going to play in Newcastle.' Stoically, she went on, 'I'll write and thank the agent, ask him if he has anything else.'

'Yeah, he might have another five-pound stand. A session with the over-sixties! I'm beginning to lose patience with you, Julie. What kind of a game are you playing? At least I know what I'm doing. I know that you can't have love and a career. Forget the Prof. Get on that piano-stool and slay them.' With a sigh, she groaned, 'I'd given up the idea of sharing your fortune but I was still hoping to bask in the glow of your success.'

'You are giving me a headache,' Julie said angrily. 'You don't know what you're talking about, Lynn. I can't help my feelings.'

'You've lost your wits, that's what is wrong with you,' Lynn snorted. 'Well, it's just another lesson to me. No man will make a fool of Lynn. I want some return for what I give. With interest.' Giving Julie another glare, she then relented and urged more gently, 'Look, think it over, Julie. Don't do anything impulsive. We'll talk about it tomorrow, when you're not so uptight.'

Touched by her friend's good will, Julie gave her a smile and reached for a cigarette. 'All right,' she agreed, 'I'll think about it.'

'If you decide to make the journey,' Lynn went on tactfully, 'I'll make it with you. And, what's more, I'll bet six to one that I sit through the whole show.'

'Performance,' Julie corrected, but already her mind was far away. So Adam was no longer engaged to Dr Tulip! If only she could play for him again! She took a deep, steadying breath and then turned to Lynn again. 'Are you in for the night?' she asked.

'I want to make a phone call, that's all,' Lynn said 'I'll be back in about ten minutes.'

'To the guy who was here?'

Lynn grinned. 'Unless I bump into something more interesting on the way.' Poking her head back through the doorway, Lynn called again, 'If you don't intend to finish that drink, pour it back. Our lifestyle may change but it hasn't yet.'

Lynn gone, Julie made herself a cup of tea. News of Adam had sent her into a spin. And now this letter from her agent! The tea made, she then switched on one of her favourite recordings, Bach's Toccata in D minor, and sat back to listen. It was great music; brave and stirring, and as usual, Julie reacted emotionally. Her lips began to tremble as she thought of Adam and she knew that she *had* to see him again. Jacques Loussier, the celebrated pianist, had made up her mind for her. She *was* going to play in Newcastle. And whether Adam was there or not, she would play for him. She would do this one concert for Adam. It could be her way of saying farewell, for each note, each cadence and chord would surely ring with the love she felt for him.

Drinking her tea quickly, Julie decided to leave a note for Lynn, telling her she could place that bet, that they were going to Newcastle. But, as she undressed for bed, she frowned anxiously again, as she imagined what the Mad Hatter of a Sister would have to say. What! Both of them off the same weekend? Impossible! But they would make it possible. At least Lynn would. Lynn would know what to do. She would possibly throw a fit or say she had eaten a bad pie and had the gallops. Snuggling beneath the bedclothes, Julie giggled happily. If Lynn had to cheat, then it would not be against her, because when she did it was always for the benefit of someone else. Lynn was like that, the most generous girl in the world. But not the most sensitive. Closing her eyes, Julie drew up her knees, then she thought of the fee she had been offered and sighed again. Life was full of surprises.

★ ★ ★ ★

'If they're paying the expenses we're not going to stay at any old bin,' Lynn asserted the following Friday night. 'I'll nip along to the phone booth and book at some highly respectable hotel. Then we'll get organised, Julie. I want to see what you're wearing for the concert.

'I've already decided,' Julie called back firmly. 'I'm wearing my cream evening gown. I like the gathered skirt and it is rather graceful. Also it's light and easy to wear.'

'You'll look like a virgin,' Lynn said, stopping in her tracks to give Julie a dubious look.

'I've made up my mind,' Julie shot back vigorously. 'Besides, how can anyone look like a virgin?'

Lynn shrugged her shoulders. 'I don't know,' she said lightly, 'but you will in that cream thing. Sort of shimmering. Still, I suppose it will be all the more of a surprise when you start pounding that piano. Keep that up and you'll have muscles like a docker.'

'Have you packed your case?' Julie asked impatiently.

'All I need will go in my tote-bag,' Lynn said. 'We should be back on Sunday. But I must get along to the phone booth. I'll book in for one night, then we shall see what turns up.'

'We should be in Newcastle by midday,' Julie called. 'We will need some lunch.'

'Okay. Leave it to me...'

A moment later the front door slammed and Julie turned to stare at her piano. There wasn't much time. In the morning they would be on their way. A wistful look in her eyes, as she sat down on her piano-stool, and soon her fingers were running over the keys and again she was lost in her playing. And as she played, she felt her heart swell with love for Adam. Again she prayed that he might be there at her concert.

'Doing your artichokes again?' Lynn

shouted as she breezed back into the room, ten minutes later. 'You may as well, you'll not get another chance. We're booked in at a four star hotel, Julie. The best I could do at such short notice.' Clapping her hands to her ears, she called again, 'Oh, give up, Julie. Have an early night. You'll damage my ear-drums.'

'I wouldn't exactly call that complimentary,' Julie flung and she suddenly stood up and shut down the piano lid. 'That's it,' she said in a positive tone. 'I won't touch it again, Lynn. And I will have an early night. What are you going to do?' Narrowing her eyes, she gave Lynn a long look and then enquired, 'You're not expecting anyone, are you? That friend, for instance?'

'Of course not!' Lynn frowned back at Julie. 'He's far enough away. I just wish he was here.'

'Then you do like him.'

'Yes,' Lynn said and she grinned self-consciously. 'I'll admit it, he is rather special. Certainly a lot different from the blokes I usually bump into. In fact, Julie, I'd like you to meet him.'

Julie gave her friend another long, amused look, then she said, 'I'm off to bed, Lynn. I'll leave you to contemplate on the fate of women foolish enough to fall in love.'

'Mad enough to let the chap know,' Lynn asserted hotly. 'That's where women make the mistake. They can't keep their mouths shut. And men are mean, quick to take advantage. I don't intend to become the biggest bargain in any bloke's life. That's what my mum said she was – the biggest bargain my dad had ever had.'

'But you do like the guy?' Julie teased round the door.

'He's great. He's fun,' Lynn called back aggressively. 'And I'm not mean with him. He can afford to pay his slaves.'

After that the flat became oddly silent, each girl lost in their own orbit of thought. Lynn sat gazing at the gas-fire while Julie lay in bed, her hands knotted behind her head, her eyes wistful.

Next morning Julie and Lynn were on the train for the north which left at eight o'clock from King's Cross. Lynn was wearing her black corduroy cat-suit over a warm cream sweater and Julie was wearing her new blue cape-style jacket over a checked skirt and shirt. They looked young and gay and, as the train moved out of the station, they smiled at each other across their small table.

'Did you sleep well?' Lynn asked.

'Not too badly,' Julie answered. 'I heard the clock strike two, then no more until you brought my cuppa.'

'It's your big day, Julie,' Lynn smiled fondly at her friend. 'And, what's more,' she said, turning to the window, 'it's a nice, bright, happy day. Everyone is in a good mood. Perhaps we're going to have an Indian summer.'

'It could be different in the north,' Julie said. 'They get a lot of cold winds up there.'

'They won't worry me,' Lynn answered and she turned back to her friend with, 'I'm going to have a look at the new shopping complex this afternoon, Julie. What are you going to do? You won't want to tire yourself.'

'There is sure to be a rehearsal,' Julie answered. 'After that, I'll take it easy.'

'Take it easy now,' Lynn suggested. 'Shut your eyes, Julie.'

At York, Julie and Lynn got out of the train to stretch their legs and buy a couple of magazines and, at twelve o'clock, they were in Newcastle. Apprehensive now, Julie picked up her case and followed Lynn across the platform to the ladies' room.

'I'll freshen up,' she said. 'I've suddenly got palpitations, Lynn. I'm scared.'

'Come on,' Lynn encouraged. 'You'll be all right. You look a bit hot but a cold wash will soon take care of that. I'll get a morning paper. There may be some mention of your concert.'

'I shouldn't think so,' Julie murmured as they marched into a large, empty waiting-room.

'Stick your case on the table,' Lynn suggested. 'I'll look after it. But hang on, I'll get a paper.'

A few moments later, Lynn was back, a smile on her face, a paper in her hand. 'Go on,' she said. 'I'm cool enough. I don't want a wash.'

Julie hurried away through another doorway and Lynn stood with her back against the table to read the paper.

'It's not bad in here,' Julie called back above the sound of running water but this time Lynn paid no attention to her friend's recommendation. Something on the second page of her paper had caught her eye. And now Lynn bit her lip painfully as she read:

Many women in the north will be both surprised and sorry to learn that the eminent gynaecologist, Professor Adam Rich, has given up his work at the city hospital and leaves for Boston, America, on Monday where he will work with a team of surgeons engaged in research...

Lynn read no more. Deliberately, she

crushed up the news sheet and, without losing a moment, hurried out on to the platform to find a rubbish bin. Julie was not to see that! Her own face stiff with shock, she returned to the waiting-room. Now *she* had palpitations.

'That's better,' said Julie as she re-appeared. 'I'm all right now, Lynn. Let's call a taxi.'

'And don't forget you've got to phone the conductor before two o'clock,' Lynn reminded as she turned quickly to the door.

'I'm hardly likely to forget that, am I?' Julie contended. 'What do you think I'm here for?'

Her lips firmly compressed, no smile on her face now, Lynn hurried ahead. She knew exactly why Julie was in Newcastle. She knew why her friend had accepted this engagement. Above everything, Julie wanted to see Adam Rich. It was this romantic notion that was keeping Julie going. One glance at that write-up and her friend would go to pieces.

'Lynn,' Julie complained as she breathlessly endeavoured to keep up with her friend, 'for goodness sake, slow down a bit. You'd think...'

Lynn was not listening. Adam Rich was leaving for Boston on Monday. That meant he could be in London already. But there was a chance that he had not left Newcastle. A remote chance but one she was not prepared to ignore. She had to do something. It was imperative.

'Look, Julie,' she said, stopping abruptly and turning to face her, yet still evading Julie's startled eyes, 'I want to make a phone call. Wait here. I'll only be a few minutes.'

'Another phone call? Oh, not now, Lynn.' Julie's expression was impatient. 'You're really chasing that...'

It was no use, Lynn was already out of hearing distance. In dismay, Julie watched her turn a corner and then she stood back against the wall, out of the way of the travellers waiting for tickets. The air was full of excitement; porters whistled, trolleys rumbled and now someone was making an announcement over the loudspeaker. Julie closed her eyes. There was a comforting smell of coffee, toasted teabuns. She thought of Adam. She had returned to Newcastle and now her heart welled with hope. He would be at the concert. She would play for him. Oh, he would be there! Firming her lips, she willed him to be.

Then Lynn came striding back, a pleased look on her face. 'I got straight through,' she called. And, striding ahead, 'Come on, I'll call a taxi.'

EIGHT

As they waited in the small dressing-room behind stage Julie told Lynn, 'I'm positively shaking. You'd think I had an overactive thyroid. Look at my hands. I'm all of a quiver.'

Lynn shrugged, this way and that. 'So what!' she said. 'You always said the best artists suffer agonies before a performance. You'll be all right, Julie. And you look great. Just like a concert pianist.' Grinning, she added, 'Cultured and intelligent but still sexy. I know you've got it made.'

'Have I?' Julie sounded a thousand miles away.

'Of course!' Lynn encouraged. 'And if you're wondering if the Prof will turn up, I'd say there was an even chance.'

'What makes you think so?' Julie said in a

wistful voice and turning to the mirror on the wall again. 'He seems to have had a change of heart. Perhaps he has also lost his love of music.'

'Well, if he hasn't the notice was in the morning paper. I saw it myself. I forgot to tell you.'

Reglossing her lips, Julie wondered if it was to be a farewell performance. A farewell to Adam. Even so, she hoped he would be there.

'Five minutes, please,' a voice called outside the door.

'Isn't this exciting,' Lynn gasped and she turned bright red.

'You had better get to your seat, Lynn,' Julie said gravely.

'Yes – good luck, Julie.' Pausing by the door to stare anxiously back at her friend, Lynn added with a brave show of light-heartedness, 'After the show we're really going to celebrate... Performance, then.' Lynn made a face. 'And don't forget to breathe in deeply,' she called. 'That should help the nerves.'

For a moment Julie turned back to the mirror to stare at the reflection of her still grave face. Then came another rap at the door, and she quickly gathered her wits.

The hall was packed and Julie walked out on to the stage to a spatter of applause from the galleries which quickly spread through the hall. The conductor drew her forward. She bowed to the audience and then took her seat at the piano. The conductor took his position in the podium. Julie waited for the cue. The house lights dimmed. And now amidst a breathless silence the first strong chords of Tchaikovsky's Concerto in B Flat minor rose to send a shudder of delight through the listeners. Julie played the *Andante maestoso* with both drive and brilliance and then the romantic section with charm and easy grace. She raised her eyes to briefly acknowledge the conductor's smile of appraisal. All was going well.

So well that Julie chanced a glance in the direction of the stalls. As usual the front row was occupied by patrons, critics, colleagues of the conductor and relatives of the musicians.

But there was Lynn. Dear Lynn, looking lovely and lost, her face rapt with anticipation. And next to Lynn? Julie swallowed hard and then looked up again. Her face worked. Impossible! She started on a downward run of notes. But it was! Herman Brook sat next to Lynn. Another brief glance told her that they were together, and very much so.

Now came in the string section, then with amazing panache Julie raised her hands ready to come in again. Adam was not there and so it was farewell. Everything went into her playing now, everything she had felt and suffered and when at last the concerto came to an end and the conductor again drew her forward, something like bedlam broke loose. At once the hall was filled with applause, applause mingled with whistles and catcalls from the younger element, who were already out in the aisles.

Fame had come, yet Julie found it impossible to smile. And as she left the stage it was not humility that bowed her head, nor were her tears tears of gladness.

'You were wonderful!' Lynn gasped as she burst into Julie's dressing room. 'Oh, Julie, I'm so proud of you.' Hugging her friend, she breathed, 'We're certainly going to celebrate.' And, dancing round the tiny room, Lynn called excitedly, 'Oh, what gorgeous flowers. And so many! Oh, Julie, you'll be famous. I'll have a famous friend.'

Her face stiff with indignation, Julie said, 'Why didn't you tell me about Herman Brook? I saw you were with him. However did you bump into him, Lynn?' And with a contemptuous glare, 'I suppose he is the fellow you've been ringing all week.'

'I didn't want to upset you.' Lynn's face creased unhappily.

'I don't like him.'

'I do,' Lynn breathed out heavily. 'Look,' she said, 'we're not going to fight. Not tonight. Besides, you didn't want him.'

'That vulgar brute turns you on?' Julie's face twisted disdainfully.

'Okay, so now you know,' Lynn shrugged. 'He does.'

'You could have told me,' Julie's voice shook.

Lynn looked steadily at her friend. 'We can't talk about it now,' she said pointedly. 'You have to go out there and face your clever friends. But I will say this, Julie, I met Herman when he came looking for you at St George's. I knew how you felt about him so when the two of us got together I found it simpler not to say anything. We went out a couple of times in Newcastle and I saw him in London before he went back to America. Now he's back in England.'

'And I suppose Herman Brook has been subsidising the rent?' Julie flung contemptuously. 'He is the friend you talked about.'

'He's a good friend, Julie,' Lynn said in a lowered tone and averting her eyes. 'More than a friend now. We've struck up an odd kind of relationship. And it's not altogether his money I'm after.' Giggling self-consciously, Lynn confessed, 'I didn't worry too much about not telling you, Julie. I knew he had trod on your toes, but, honestly, he doesn't offend me. That's because I'm not in love with anyone else.'

'Well,' Julie said furiously, 'it's your life to throw away if you want to. I found him – two stone overweight.'

Lynn did not laugh this time, she screwed up her face and said soberly, 'At least I now understand how you feel about the Prof.'

Adam! Julie suddenly covered her face with her hands. 'Oh, Lynn,' she said brokenly, 'I did want to see him. I was so sure he would be here. I was so disappointed.'

'I must say you covered it beautifully,' Lynn encouraged. 'Honestly, you were wonderful. And you had better get out there because everyone will be wanting to congratulate you.' Biting her lip, Lynn stared hard at Julie. Then she went on,

'Herman has some news for you, Julie. He is waiting to see you.'

Turning away, Julie wished that Adam Rich was waiting to see her, and again she bowed her head and tears came to her eyes. Then she heard Lynn calling excitedly.

'Hi, Julie, have you seen this?'

'What?' Julie swung round.

'This card on the bouquet of roses. It's from the Prof!' And with a contemptuous sniff, 'Trust a surgeon to send ruddy roses.'

'I don't believe you,' Julie said on a quick intake of breath, and with trembling fingers, she turned up the card. And instantly the colour flooded up from her throat and the tears she had suppressed now flowed freely.

Red roses from Adam! But his note was brief. 'Good luck, Julie,' it read, 'Adam.' Then he had known she was playing in Newcastle that night. And if he had been unable to attend the performance he had at least cared enough to send a bouquet. 'Oh, Lynn,' Julie breathed, 'They are from Adam. They are! He has not forgotten me.'

'Pity,' Lynn shrugged. 'You could have had lots of dates tonight. There's nothing like success for making a woman look sexy.'

'I must go,' Julie said breathlessly. 'You will tell Herman to join the party, Lynn. I'll be delighted to see him.' Her face radiant, she went on wildly, 'Adam may still turn up, Lynn. And, oh, if only he would.'

Lynn followed Julie out and soon Julie was mingling with the other musicians, who were noisily chatting with their friends and relatives. A journalist with a bushy beard and bright, probing eyes began to pester her and then the conductor swept her away to someone he was anxious for her to meet. But even then a young and very flushed girl managed to stop them and ask for Julie's autograph. Blushing as hard as the young girl, Julie signed the brandished programme.

It was a noisy party, everyone drinking, everyone chatting non-stop on the platform which they were using for their after-concert celebration. Everyone greeted Julie with smiles of appraisal, and compliments fell like blessings on her ears.

Then Lynn appeared again and this time Herman was with her.

'Julie!' he boomed as they came towards her. 'I'm sure proud of you, little lady. Goddam it, one of these days it will be a Command Performance! And I'll be there. That's a promise. Herman will be there.'

Taut with embarrassment, Julie gave him a smile. For Lynn's sake she had to be nice to Herman. 'Thank you,' she murmured. Then laughing a little, she went on, 'I must say I'm surprised to see you, Herman. But pleased, too.'

'Then we'll kiss and make up?'

Julie smiled again, at the same time as she took a step back.

'Herman, get to the point,' Lynn insisted. 'Julie's got to mingle and you did say we were doing the clubs.'

'I won't keep you long, honey,' Herman said and he reached out to squeeze Lynn's hand and draw her to him. 'Nor you, Julie.

But I have news for you.'

'News?' Julie's throat worked.

And then a young man with long hair and wearing steel-rimmed glasses pushed in rudely and said, 'Someone has suggested that you will be the next Eileen Joyce, Miss Singer. Have you any comment?'

Julie had not, but Lynn had. 'Buzz off,' she snapped, and the astonished journalist did.

'What news, Herman?' Julie began again, her eyes seeking his.

'Go on, Herman,' Lynn urged. 'Don't keep her in suspense. Besides, we're getting unpopular.' Under her breath she explained, 'Everyone wants a word with this famous woman.'

'Here goes then,' Herman began and he squared his shoulders and took a deep breath before he told Julie, 'I've been to see your lawyers, Julie. And to come to the point, they have decided to let you have half of that legacy your uncle left you.'

'Half?' Julie backed back, shock and confusion registering on her flushed face.

'Well, honey, you did manage to get through about half of that goddam training. That's what Herman had to point out. And they listened. They were goddam sympathetic.' Smiling, he added, 'They also knew the old boy.'

'You did this for me?' Julie's throat worked again, she exchanged glances with Lynn.

'Let's say I did penance,' Herman grinned and he gave Julie a wink. 'So there we are, honey. You'll not be wealthy but you will be able to go on with your studies. And, having known your late uncle so well, I can safely say he would approve of this codicil.'

The room swam. Julie reached for Herman's arm. 'I can't believe it,' she murmured. 'Oh, Herman, how can I ever repay you. I thought the solicitors had decided against letting me have anything. And then there was Lynn's letter. I suppose she has told you how she forged Matron's signature?'

'She did?' Herman's large face seemed to blow up and deflate again. 'And she got away with it,' he roared. 'She's some girl, eh, Julie?'

'You are some man,' Julie breathed. 'You are absolutely wonderful.'

'He is, isn't he?' Lynn agreed readily, beaming at her man. 'But you'll have to get the details later, Julie. We'd better go. And you'd better mingle, Julie. We're getting some rather nasty looks.'

'There should be a letter for you on Monday,' Herman said as he put his arm across Lynn's shoulders. 'Keep your fingers crossed.'

'Come on, Herman.'

'I'm coming, honey.' Glancing back, Herman smiled again as he called, 'And congratulations again, Julie. That playing was great. I even knew the tune. Tra, la, lar, lar ... boom, boom. Very romantic!'

A look of disbelief still on her face, Julie watched them go: her lovable friend Lynn and Herman Brook. Herman, vulgar no doubt, insensitive but good-humoured and generous to a fault. And Lynn making the most of her remarkable find. Her head spinning, Julie at last turned to face the little groups of people still waiting to have a word with her. And now she could tell them. She was going back to the London College of Music. She would one day be a real concert pianist. One perhaps known all over the world! But again her gaze ran over the platform and she sighed involuntarily, for there was still no sign of Adam. And something told her that he was already far, far away.

★ ★ ★ ★

'Look,' Lynn said the following night after Herman had driven them back to the south, 'Herman has a flight back to America on Monday, Julie, so I may be late. Very late. So don't you forget to lock up. Don't take any chances. You hear too many nasty things. In fact, I wouldn't leave you on your own, Julie, but he is going away...'

'Be careful, Lynn,' Julie said frowning

slightly. 'I suggest you get back for a few hours' sleep. We are on duty in the morning. And I don't fancy facing the Mad Hatter alone.'

'You don't need to face her,' Lynn said as she touched up her make-up and squinted through the mirror at Julie. 'You'll have that letter in the morning, so why go back at all.'

'Don't be ridiculous,' Julie retaliated indignantly. 'I must at least work a week's notice.'

'I'm glad I have no qualms of conscience,' Lynn laughed back. 'Herman just needs to say the word.' Zipping up her skirt, she grinned at Julie again. 'Oh, that reminds me,' she added, 'if I don't happen to turn up would you take some talc in for Mrs Fox. We've got stones of the stuff.'

'And she hasn't a soul in the world, I know.'

'I'm off, then.' Lynn picked up her jacket and bag. 'Now don't forget,' she said again. 'Lock up.' At the door she called back impishly, 'And don't worry about me. What harm could a girl come to with a guy like Herman?'

Julie regarded her friend silently for a few moments, then she said, 'You are in love, Lynn. I can hardly believe it, but you are.'

Lynn grinned again. 'I'm in love with his money and I like his manicured nails,' she teased. 'But I don't intend to go all soulful. There's a good film on telly, Julie. And you should have the letter from your solicitors in the morning, so don't you sit moping. To hell with Adam Rich. You've got a career.' At the door she glanced back again to shout, 'And don't forget, I'll be late. Very late, so don't start ringing the police.'

Julie gave Lynn a long, grave look, then she said pointedly, 'All right, Lynn, I'll see you tomorrow. I get the message.'

Another grin and Lynn was gone. And as the front door slammed shut Julie got the feeling that she was the only one left in the world.

And there were Adam's red roses.

Julie stood staring down at them for a long

time. Adam was gone, she knew it, and she felt as though her heart would surely break. Despair, loneliness engulfed her.

And then, quite suddenly, an idea came to Julie, the impact of which sent her hurtling out on to the landing. She picked up her coat and then hurried downstairs and out into the night. The phone box was only a hundred yards or so down the street. And she had to make a phone call!

Her heart pounding with excitement, Julie dialled a Newcastle number, then she stood back to wait.

The voice came, a familiar one that made Julie catch her breath. It was Sister Grey and she said in her usual shrill voice, 'Ward Eleven, this is Sister Grey speaking. Can I help you?'

'Sister Grey!' Julie fought to disguise her voice. Her heart was hammering dangerously, her hands trembling visibly. 'This is a friend of Professor Rich speaking. I've just got back from America. I've been ringing the Professor's home, but, unhappily, I can't

267

get a reply. It occurred to me that you might well be able to tell me where I can get in touch with the Professor. I would so much like to see him before he leaves for Boston.'

'Oh, that's a pity,' Sister Grey shrilled back. 'The Professor left on Saturday. Maureen went with him. I expect they intend to have a day or two in London together before he leaves. We're all sorry.'

'Thank you, Sister. I'm sorry to have troubled you.' Julie put the receiver down, then her face ashen with shock she staggered back to the flat like someone drugged.

'Fool! Fool!' Julie suddenly wailed with despair. Picking up a cushion she hurled it across the room in a demonstration of frustration. Adam had not only gone but he had taken someone called Maureen with him. Sobbing now, Julie picked up the cushion and pressing it to the wall she hid her face in it. She had imagined herself to be the only woman in love with Adam and now she realised that there could have been quite a queue of lovesick women ready to take Susie Tulip's place. Another sob, another sigh and Julie decided to fix herself on of Lynn's corpse revivers. She did feel deathly. Shocked and as though everything in her stomach had turned to stone.

Adam was gone. Gone for ever.

And it was dark outside and too silent in the flat. She wished Lynn had not gone out for the night. Without realising it she switched on the telly, then she went to the window and peered out, her face set with sadness, her hand on the curtain still trembling.

She would never see Adam Rich again.

Standing stiffly by the window, Julie fought to make plans for her future. She had every chance now to become a celebrated concert pianist. Her career would be uncluttered, she would be single-minded. Also she would write to her mother at once, giving her the good news. Her mother would be able to give up her job and spend more time with her young brother. And all thanks to Herman Brook.

But she could not stop thinking about Adam. She could not stop torturing herself. Who was Maureen? Where were they? And why had he sent her red roses? Each thought brought a fresh rush of anguish. By ten o'clock a numbing despair had settled upon Julie and she was glad to go to bed and turn out the light. Thank God for sleep, she thought...

But sleep did not last long. And now a strange little scraping noise held Julie riveted. Only her throat worked with fear as she again strained her ears. It came again, the same scraping sound. And it came from somewhere in the flat! Somewhere quite close.

Had she locked the door? Julie's heart leapt up with a fresh surge of fear, for she knew she had not. But if she had not, surely an intruder would walk straight in. Nibbling her underlip nervously, Julie knew she must investigate. Then she thought she heard a footstep, and in a flash she was up and reaching for her dressing-gown. She would not be trapped in the flat, she had to get downstairs, outside ... shout for help if necessary. Run to the booth, telephone 999. She was sure now that there was someone in the flat and she was not just going to lie there waiting to be murdered in her bed.

The street was ominously silent, deserted. But, no, a long, low car was making it's way slowly along by the kerb, the driver peering out of the window at each doorway. Julie held her breath, then back in again. Then came a crash from upstairs and with a cry of alarm Julie bounded out on to the pathway.

The long, low car had stopped. Someone was getting out. Julie was about to call for help but she now stopped in her tracks and lips parted and her eyes widened in amazement. Adam! She went on staring, transfixed, disbelievingly. It was!

'Julie!'

She could only stare at him. She wanted to say something but no sound would come from her lips.

'Well, you damn well took some finding,' Adam said in a low voice, the light of triumph in his eyes. 'Julie ... there is so much I want to say.'

'Adam,' she whispered, blinking back her tears, 'you were looking for me?'

His hand cupped her elbow. 'Aren't you going to invite me in?'

'Of course,' she gasped incredulously. 'This way,' she added a little drunkenly.

In the small sitting-room upstairs they faced each other and, after a long, tense silence, Julie asked, 'How did you get my address?' And because he was looking at her in such a wonderful way, and because he was even more darkly handsome than she remembered, she felt herself falling in love with him all over again. And she turned away because she suddenly remembered the gentleness of his clever hands, the firm strength of his mouth. 'How did you know..?' Her voice shook, she could not go on.

'I got your address from Sister Grey,'

Adam said gently reaching out to draw Julie back to face him. 'Apparently, your friend had written asking for a reference. A ridiculous letter apparently, but, thank God, giving all the news. Then, Julie,' he said on a sigh, and looking deep into her eyes, 'I received your telegram. I just wish I could have been there, but it did come a little late. I just managed to send that bouquet.'

'I got your roses, Adam,' Julie murmured.

'And their message, I hope.' His dark eyes searched to the depths of Julie's.

Telegram? Julie's heart suddenly fluttered in her chest. Which telegram? Her thoughts buzzed madly. She did not understand. She had sent no telegram. Then it came to her in a flash, an angry flash. *Lynn had sent Adam a telegram!* So that was what Lynn had been up to that morning in the station. But what had she said? Julie swallowed over a lump in her throat, then in dismay, her hand rose to cover her mouth.

'Julie...?'

'Can I get you a drink?' she asked, fighting

to make her voice sound normal.

'No, my darling, you cannot,' Adam said determinedly. 'We have too much to say to each other.'

His voice was warm and intimate and it sent a shudder of happiness through Julie. Tears again trembled on her lashes and she had to turn away.

'Julie,' he went on in a deep, husky voice now, 'how can I tell you? How can I explain? I can only say that I feel as though I had been in exile. A wanderer between heaven and earth. Without you, Julie, I was lost. Julie, I love you! You know I do!' And on a sigh he added with a touching truculence, 'Not for one damned moment have I stopped worrying about you.'

Her face suffused with happiness, her eyes shining, Julie listened to words more precious, more evoking than even her most wonderful parallel fifths or Bachian chords. Thrilled, she listened as Adam went on, 'I had to break my engagement to Susie. I knew it could never work. And to my shame she did confess that she had put the pressure on you, Julie. And when I stormed out from the Lecture Hall that night, I also knew a moment of truth. I knew I loved you, Julie.'

A pang of sadness registered on Adam's handsome face and Julie caught her breath. There was a long, tense moment of silence as they gazed at each other, then she was fast in his arms.

'I'm going to Boston for three weeks,' he told her in a voice deep with emotion. 'When I return, will you marry me, Julie? Will you love me?'

Struggling free, Julie moistened her lips and regarded him more thoughtfully, 'I also have a confession,' she said quietly, 'I rang Sister Grey on Ward Eleven. I just had to know where you were.'

'And she told you I was in London. With my sister? My youngest sister?'

'Maureen?'

'Yes,' he answered impatiently and he reached out to draw Julie close again. 'Have you anything else to confess?' he teased tenderly.

'Yes,' Julie said, struggling free again. 'There is something else, Adam. At least, someone else.'

His eyes narrowed as he drew up, squared his shoulders.

'The American.'

'Is he still around?' Adam's voice was harsh.

'Very much so,' Julie laughed, having enjoyed the momentary deception. 'He's with my friend, Lynn. They really make a pair, Adam. Lynn is quite crazy and Herman is most vulgar but, apart from these failings, they are the two most human beings I know. And, what's more, I'd say it was an even bet that Lynn will return to America with Herman. She's a wonderful girl, Adam. She's alive, Adam. Not clever but certainly cunning. Lynn's not one for dreaming.'

'I suddenly like her,' Adam teased, his dark eyes merry again. 'I like her a lot.'

As he spoke he reached out to Julie again but this time she drew back and went on determinedly, 'Adam, I must tell you about Herman Brook. I want you to like him too. Or at least appreciate what he has done for me.'

'What has he done for you?' Adam's throat worked as he straightened up.

'Herman was a friend of my late uncle's, Adam,' Julie explained quickly and with a hint of aggression. 'And, believe me, dear Herman is not so insensitive as we made him out to be. He actually went back to America and persuaded my uncle's solicitors to let me have part of the legacy which had been left to me with that dreadful proviso. So, you see, Adam, I can now go back to my studies. I may yet fulfil my dream and become a famous concert pianist.'

For a moment a silence like a barrier came down between them, a silence broken at last by Adam's long sigh. Then, reaching to take Julie's hand in his own, he searched her flushed face with tender eyes. 'You will indeed,' he said in a voice which ran over Julie like thick, warm honey. 'You will be a famous pianist, my darling. I always knew you would be.' Another pause and then taking Julie's other hand he drew her close. 'Your talent is for the world, Julie,' he whispered with emotion. 'But your love that is what I need. I want you so much. I love you so much.'

Through a haze of happiness, Julie murmured, 'You did love Susie.'

'Never!' he answered shortly, momentarily drawing back. 'I was attracted to Susie. I even admired her. But from the moment you walked into my theatre I cared about you, Julie. I couldn't stop caring, being concerned for you. I felt responsible for you. I wanted to be. I never cared for Susie ... in such a way. I never loved Susie in such a manner. And I do love you, Julie. I love you and I want you.'

Julie bowed her head and then laid her cheek against his shoulder. 'Oh, Adam,' she whispered, 'Oh, Adam, I love you so much. I had to leave St George's because of you. I was prepared to give up my legacy because of you. Then, after that awful scene in the Lecture Hall, I knew that you would never believe me. You despised me. I saw it in your eyes.'

'How blind can a man be,' he murmured against her hair. 'Oh, Julie, thank God I found you.'

Again, in silence, they gazed into each other's eyes. Soon he would have to go and their heart beats cruelly ticked away the time.

'Kiss me,' Julie breathed desperately. 'Oh, Adam, kiss me.'

He kissed her gently this time, then again and again until Julie suddenly struggled free and gasped, 'Must you go? Must you go so soon, Adam? I don't want you to leave me.'

He wanted to make love to her and suddenly he reached out for her. She heard again the wild pounding of his heart so close to her own. Again they clung to each other, stared again at each other in new and silent understanding.

'I must go, my darling,' he said firmly. 'Don't make it harder for me.'

'Oh, Adam!' Julie clung to him again, frantically this time. 'Must you go tonight?' she burst out.

He did not answer her but Julie caught the flash of joy in his eyes and heard again the wild pounding of his heart so close to her own. Again they clung to each other, stared again at each other in new and silent understanding.

'All right,' Julie whispered at last, half teasingly, half despairingly. 'You don't want me tonight.'

'No,' he said as he smoothed her hair back from her brow and then gently kissed it. 'I don't want you tonight, Julie. I want you for ever.' And raising her chin he looked into her china-blue eyes again and, smiling, he asked, 'Will you marry me, Julie? Will you marry me the moment, the very moment I get back?'

Julie could not answer him, suddenly there was the most wonderful, most perfect music in her heart. She managed to nod her head in assent and raise her lips to Adam's again. It seemed that all her dreams were coming true. There was such gentleness in his eyes... And she could not help herself, she returned his kiss with a fresh surge of passion.

The publishers hope that this book has given you enjoyable reading. Large Print Books are especially designed to be as easy to see and hold as possible. If you wish a complete list of our books please ask at your local library or write directly to:

Dales Large Print Books
Magna House, Long Preston,
Skipton, North Yorkshire.
BD23 4ND

This Large Print Book for the partially sighted, who cannot read normal print, is published under the auspices of
THE ULVERSCROFT FOUNDATION

THE ULVERSCROFT FOUNDATION

... we hope that you have enjoyed this Large Print Book. Please think for a moment about those people who have worse eyesight problems than you ... and are unable to even read or enjoy Large Print, without great difficulty.

You can help them by sending a donation, large or small to:

The Ulverscroft Foundation, 1, The Green, Bradgate Road, Anstey, Leicestershire, LE7 7FU, England.
or request a copy of our brochure for more details.

The Foundation will use all your help to assist those people who are handicapped by various sight problems and need special attention.

Thank you very much for your help.

Other DALES Titles
In Large Print

JANIE BOLITHO
Wound For Wound

BEN BRIDGES
Gunsmoke Is Grey

PETER CHAMBERS
A Miniature Murder Mystery

CHRISTOPHER CORAM
Murder Beneath The Trees

SONIA DEANE
The Affair Of Doctor Rutland

GILLIAN LINSCOTT
Crown Witness

PHILIP McCUTCHAN
The Bright Red Business